MW00961135

DEDICATION

This book is dedicated to the following: Don Noble, the man who started it all and was kind enough to bring me in to Riot Forge. Kevin Candela, Kent Hill, and Jeff O'Brien who I have learned from along the way and have helped me when I was stuck. To my wife Krystal and our kids who are patient with me while I spend most of my free time working on this stuff. And to my oldest daughter Adriana, who is starting to enjoy the scarier things in life. Here are some stories you could probably read, except mine, you'll have to be eighteen for that one.

CONTENTS

The Classics Never Die!

FOREWORD

Ever since I was a teenager I loved horror movies. Especially the slashers and gore films such as Friday the 13th, Nightmare On Elm Street, and of course Halloween. Dario Argento, and Lucio Fulci films were also favorites. Classics like Evil Dead, Dawn Of The Dead, and Dead Alive. But there was a part of me that also enjoyed the old, quieter, atmosphere of the black and white films of yore.

Frankenstein

Dracula

Wolf man

Creature From the Black Lagoon

I remember being very young and watching The Creature From The Black Lagoon with 3D glasses at home with my family and being pretty terrified of it. Years later I watched Frankenstein (still have my DVD copy with all the sequels) and Wolfman. And I'm sure at some point Creature again but less terrified this time.

So my brother and I had this idea. What if we put together a collection of these classic monsters only with a more modern, bizarre twist to them? He had written a novella featuring Dracula's brother who has ADHD and we thought how about we do something like that. Put a new spin on some old favorites. Thus the book you have in your hands was born.

Within these pages you'll find Dracula, only connected to a more real life series of crimes. A biker Creature From The Black Lagoon. The Invisible Man as secret agent, and many more new ideas on old favorites.

Twists on these characters have been done before in movies like Frankenstein Conquers the World, cartoons like Alvin and the Chipmunks meet The Wolfman, and even a few musicals. But the authors in these pages have created something brand new and unique. Shown in ways you've probably never even thought of before. No matter what shape or form they come writers will find new ways to make them interesting.

After all these years, decades even, it seems these monsters will always be a part of our culture. Whether it's in movies, books, or games, the classics never die.

EDWARD VAUGHN, JULY, 2017

Foreward

The seed of the idea for this anthology came about after I had read Jeff Burk's Cripplewolf, which is a Bizarro novella about a guy in a wheel chair that turns into a werewolf. While taking one of Garrett Cook's online classes I thought about Cripplewolf and made up my own Bizarro version of a classic movie monster with my novella The ADHD Vampire. Years later my brother Edward and I got to talking about how cool it would be to have an anthology of new and interesting takes on the classic monsters. We could do what Jeff and I did with those creatures but get others involved and have a bunch of awesome stories using all the monsters. Both of us had been involved with Riot Forge and The Baum Ass Stories anthologies Zeb Carter put together so we figured we could just follow in his foot steps. Being on the other side of the production of an anthology was new to both of us and I think its safe to say we learned a lot. This project ended up taking longer than intended for various reasons but I'm grateful that all of the authors involved understood and continued their support for this. We assembled some great writers who brought some fantastic stories. Their love for the classic monsters show in their work. If you love all these monsters too then I believe you're in for a real treat!

MATTHEW VAUGHN, JULY, 2017

WHERE THE STREETS ARE PAVED WITH BLOOD

BY: JODIE MANNING-BARES

Ah, Whitechapel. What filth. I had thought my ancient eyes had seen the worst of horrors in many battles, and in my own fields of impaled Turkish prisoners that lined my castle's landscape—and yet, Whitechapel. If one is not careful you will die from just inhaling it's stench of decomposing human excrement and immoralities. Not that it is any of my concern. Why, I remember as if it happened only yesterday. Turn one corner in Whitechapel and you are the pride of the whores. Those horrid ladies of the night throwing their disgusting skirted frames at any male passerby. They look not for love, but for enough money to carry them to the next pub for the availability of their sustenance—alcohol. The next street over, one may find himself part of the underground world of gambling. One might place his bet on how long a man may last in a match of fisticuffs, or, a new trend where the so called upper class "gentlemen" bet on how many rats a dog can throttle in a minute. How little did they know that they were the rats to our kind? When my companions and I first arrived, we were unsure that London would suit our needs, yet we came to find out that nobody is missed in Whitechapel. One simply vanishes into the thick foggy London streets.

I had never been to London before. I am used to the countryside of Transylvania. I remember fondly the days when the corpses of the fallen lined the green rolling hills. When one could merely slip into the shadows and feed freely without any family coming to claim the bodies. How savage we were then, even the most civilized of us. The gypsies even kept away from our kind. All except one. She had the most piercing gray eyes, like the finest stone of a fortification. Her auburn hair swirled around her thin shoulders, making it look as if a nasty sea creature constantly clung to her. She was never frightened of me when I came to call. She took it as affection that I chose her over the other maidens in her caravan. I never knew her real name then, but when I turned her I named her Garnet, after the color of her sweet satisfying blood. For a time, it was her gentle caress that soothed the savage beast inside of me. We fed together, we formed a union, but it was Garnet who was eager to get away from Transylvania.

Of course, we could not travel alone. Two night-walkers could not manage so long a journey on their own. That is when having a man comes in handy. That man is Crispin, a young Roman I keep in my company. He owes me a life debt after I saved him from the silver bullet of an irate farmer. Crispin is a werewolf and though the tales of the vampire/werewolf relationship are regarded with vicious rumors of hate and jealousy, Crispin and I have found affection. In fact, I often find myself lost in wonderment at him. His eyes, pools of deep blue that rival the mightiest seas. His neatly clipped chestnut hair, except for the long strain of white that hangs against his rugged proud jawline. His lips that quiver when he calls me master. Oh, how I adore these two. If my heart could beat, it would sing out their praises.

Garnet was the mastermind in plotting our trip to London. For a woman, she is well versed in how to manage procuring transport for travel. It seems I have taught her well, and with good reason too. Soon she will take on her own progeny, meaning she will turn a mortal into one of us thus becoming his or her mate, and leave my company for some period of time. It is a fairly common thing among our kind. Since we live such longer existences than humans, we are free to set our own standards on "companionship." Garnet has been with me nearly a hundred and fifty years now, a ripe time for a young one to step into their own. Our contract of companionship was made out within those parameters. However, it is not uncommon for our kind to rekindle companionship later on, or as in my present case, have more than one they consider companions.

Garnet came up with the brilliant plan of having Crispin offer a cargo ship captain double his current transport price to bring two coffins and himself, a passenger, to London. Crispin is a convincing orator, to add to his repertoire of skills. He sold the captain the story that the coffins contained the bodies of two soldiers from the Crusades that had been found in an unmarked grave adorned in the fashion of those great battles. They were to be returned back to their native land and buried in a memorial plot for the family crests reflected upon their shields. Without a moment to spare, we were on our way to London arriving on the eve of 20th of August.

We found pitiful but secure lodging at a hovel of a hotel within the district of Whitechapel. It was nothing compared to the luxury of Bran castle back home. However, this particular lodge had underground rooms, so it fit our needs perfectly. Even in the light of day, being underground we could walk the corridors and size up our potential prey. It was pretty evident from the first night that there was a favorite Whitechapel pass time. We could hear the woman's pleasured screams before we reached them in the corridor.

"Look at this," Garnet spat at me. "Have people no shame that they just throw themselves at each other in a corridor? Can they not even find a bed or a pile of hay?"

I laughed at her disgust.

"Oh, my darling. You worry about the decency of their love making practices, and yet you think they would not scoff or shriek at our own practices?" I asked as we entered our room.

"We would at least put on a good show, whereas this is disgusting filth and depravity. These so called women throwing themselves at any man like an animal in heat. No offense, Crispin."

"None taken," our werewolf companion replied in his heavily Italian accented voice. "They are only acting as such because we are in the prime area that prostitutes troll for johns, or so I was told by the innkeeper. He inquired if I were looking for local entertainment."

"Well then," Garnet replied, "that is why they have no shame. I wish the world could be rid of people like them. The scum of the earth that relies solely upon their vices."

I laughed again.

"Garnet, have you forgotten what you are, my dear? You have no shame of feeding on a person and often times killing them. You are not much different from those women you see lining the streets. You both kill with pleasure."

She scowled at me. Her cold granite eyes boring

into my cold innards.

"I am not like those women. Those women are the types that gives gypsies a bad name. Exotic men think we are nothing but vagabonds living in mortal sin and that we are more than willing to accept them into our beds. I would love to rid the planet of those type of women."

That is when the idea struck me.

"Why don't we?" I asked my companions.

"You mean we actually kill the local hookers?" Crispin didn't bother to mask the shock in his reply.

"Yes. Do you think this place truly keeps track of those workers? Do you think those lot have families? They are choosing that profession for a reason. They are desperate. I say, let us feed on the sewer rats of Whitechapel."

"And how would we do that," Crispin wondered out loud. "You cannot just drain the hookers of their blood as you would in the countryside. There are coppers here that would be suspicious. We would have to make it look like....like murder."

"That is not half bad, my pet," I said stroking one of my long nails across his bristled cheek, *"We could stage a series of murders. We could challenge the great Scotland Yard and see if they are really the world's best police force, as they boast."*

"And perhaps, find my progeny in the process," Garnet added.

We took a few days getting to know Whitechapel and what it had to offer our kind.

When we are not actively feeding, often times we will take a little blood from Crispin to satisfy us. We studied the twists and turns of the maze like streets. We fought off hookers and beggars who looked more like specters than human beings. I was beginning to see what Garnet saw in these walking meat sacks--they were better off dead.

For the first few nights of our Whitechapel stake out, Garnet posed as a whore. She was reluctant to do so at first, but in the end agreed for the sake of the mission. The wonderful thing about being a vampire is that we can glamour a person, meaning, we have the ability to influence a human's mind to do as we please. During that time, no man was able to charm Garnet's willingness—she simply willed them away. But on the night of 30th of August, the mission began. Garnet came running to us on Durward Street, known as Buck's Row to the locals.

"I have found the first candidate," she announced, "There's a homely little whore around the corner. Her name is Mary Ann Nichols, but they call her Polly. She is a drunkard apparently, having favored her drink over a bed. I think she would be a perfect trial run."

"Show her to me," I said.

Garnet took me around the corner where I spied a woman with greasy dark hair, sunken eyes, and a sickeningly white complexion. I turned my eyes on Crispin, who met mine with a nod of agreement. Polly Nichols would be the first kill.

The next evening, the 31st of August, a full moon night, Polly Nichols was coming down Durward Street drunk on her own laughter and whiskey. She had just been turned out of a flop house for not having enough money. Pity. I hid in the shadows with Crispin in his full wolf form. As a vampire, my mind can keep him glamoured-- It is when I let up does he attack. Garnet approached her first, appearing from the shadows.

"Shame of being turned out, love" she said sweetly to Nichols.

"Baw. Ain't nothin' but a bed. Perfectly good places 'round 'ere to flop for a night. Not to worry though, love. Soon as I get me new bonnet, I'll be making the good change, me."

"I am certain you will, Polly," replied Garnet with a widening smile.

I watched as the dimples prickled at the corners of her mouth. That was the signal. I let my mind free Crispin from his telepathic hold, watching as he ran out into the street pouncing on Nichols forcing the whore to the ground. The wind was knocked from her lungs as she hit the cobbled stone street. While Crispin's sharp canines stripped away at the flesh of Nichols's torso, Garnet and I cut two deep incisions into her throat. Nichols gagged and choked as her own blood poured from the *coup de gras*, her alerting screams suppressed.

"As they say in London, cheers, love," I smirked at Garnet.

Together we bent down and started to drink greedily, savoring the warm liquid splashing against our tongues, the hue turning our lips crimson. As Mary Ann Nichols gurgled her final breath, Garnet and I kissed passionately, rolling our tongues across one another's. My fingers intertwined her auburn locks as I moaned into her mouth. It was pure bliss. However, not but a short moment later, we heard nearing voices. I ordered Crispin telepathically to run into the underground tunnels and made Garnet go with him. I stayed and slipped into the shadows admiring our work. It was beautiful, almost reminiscent of my impaling days.

For a few days after, we religiously checked the local newspapers to see if our task had made headlines. Of course, our deed went unnoticed, as does many things in Whitechapel. What is the murder of one little whore when there are so many other atrocities to cover?

"We must try again," I said to my companions, inside the comfort of our underground suite.

"Was one murder not enough for you, master?" Crispin asked as he sat beside me at a small table.

"This one was not significant enough to get the public's full attention," I replied, reaching over to caress his cheek, *"We must go at it again, and make the next one much more noticeable."*

"Why not just try the same modus operandi as before, master?" he quivered against my touch, "If we leave the same calling card, then they will link the murders."

I went quiet for the moment, carefully considering what my darling wolf-man was saying to me. He had a point. The young thing that he is, we wanted the Yard to think the same person was offing local prostitutes one after another.

"I have decided that you are right, my young one. We shall talk to Garnet and set a date for the next execution. We will not need a fresh corpse to feed on for at least a week. We will commence then."

"Yes, Master," Crispin replied turning his gaze into my cold eyes.

My mustache curled upwards as my hand came to a rest against his warm skin.

"The only caveat to consider is that I think you should lure in the next victim, Crispin. If we continue to use Garnet, people will become suspicious of her."

"I shall do as you wish, master. Though I will not be in my wolf form, I shall bring my serrated knife to do the chopping."

"And to think you were nearly ended by a farmer's bullet. Let no one say that you are not intelligent, my young one."

The night of September 8th, 1888, the second murder took place in the backyard of 29 Hanbury Street. Crispin wore a deer stalker hat and a long overcoat as he approached the unsuspecting Annie Chapman. As he distracted the pathetic whore, Garnet and I swooped from the roof tops, landing behind her and slitting her throat with a swift swipe of our nails. She dropped to the ground where Crispin sprang into action. He took his serrated knife and plunged it deep into Chapman's abdomen, working quickly to cut and sever vital organs. Garnet and I feasted upon the dying woman like a pack of wolves upon a cow. It was not but minutes until she, like Mary Nichols before her, had gargled her last breath. As the three of us turned from the scene, I noticed a leather apron hanging from the back of a door and swiftly decided to place it at the scene. I felt that surely this murder would make the morning post.

Sure enough in the following days, my companions and I were riveted with the tale in the post of the Leather Apron murderer, which was rumored to be a local Jewish man. Other arrests were made during that time, but what the Yard did not realize is that the men they held behind steel bars were indeed innocent, and we, the guilty party still roamed the streets freely. Once the appeal of the Leather Apron story wore off, the three of us felt that Whitechapel needed to be rocked by yet another murder, only we would attempt to do two in one night. Garnet had long complained about this particular whore by the name of Elizabeth Stride butting in on all the seemingly decent gentlemen she had encountered during her nightly walks. She told us how Stride had been rather cruel and how Garnet had to hold back as to not kill the bitch out in the open.

"She's next," Garnet announ-ced to Crispin and I, "If I lose the chance at another potential progeny at her hands, I think I will have to kill her solo."

"Fear not, my pet," I assured her, *"Crispin shall pose as a potential suitor for you, and we will let Stride come to us."*

On the 29th of September, Garnet was stationed just outside of the International Working Men's Educational Club talking to Crispin, putting on a good act for anyone who was watching. Hell, they even convinced me and I knew both had no real romantic interest in each other. Just then, a woman appeared and sauntered right up to where Garnet was standing with Crispin. I heard little of the conversation. I simply let myself observe the scene unfolding before my eyes. I saw Crispin holding Elizabeth Stride's arms behind her back as Garnet came forward. Her swipe was quick, almost as if she had not sliced at all at the woman, but suddenly, red streams of blood poured from Stride's throat.

"Are you not going to feed, Garnet?" Crispin asked.

"I would rather eat cyanide than taste the taint from that whore," she spat, "Leave her. Let us be off."

Crispin dropped Stride's body to the ground, leaving her suffocating upon her own blood. They walked into the shadows where they met me. I was smiling in admiration of my young ones.

"We shall celebrate your first kill as a duo," said I. *"Let us retire to the opium den down the way."*

About an hour after Stride lay dead, we were coming out of the opium den with a renewed sense of deviance. High on the best of the Orient, we were walking near Mitre Square in London. I spotted her first. She was drunk and begging every man that passed for a chance to raise a little money for a bed. We let Crispin approach her first.

"Oh please, kind sir," the woman slurred. "I will give you all of me if just for a few shillings for a bed."

"I do believe I can help you find some rest, Madame," Crispin said to her.

She did not notice that his eyes lifted from her face to over her shoulder. I swooped in like a bat, slashing her throat with my nails. Garnet came be-hind me and slashed at the woman's face. Crispin went to work with his knife, becoming an expert butcher. He removed her intestines and flung them carelessly over the woman's shoulder. A small amount of festering human excrement smeared her dress. The distant shine of a lantern and an ap-proaching carriage drew our attention quickly.

"Master," Crispin whispered loudly, "we must go. The work is not done, but we are certain to be the talk of Whitechapel come the morn."

I nodded and drug Garnet away from the dying woman. We would not know until the next morning that the woman that died at Mitre Square was named Catherine Eddowes.

The details of the murders of both Elizabeth Stride and Catherine Eddowes were plastered over the pages of every newspaper outlet in London. Scotland Yard did not know what to make of it. They assumed they had their man responsible for all the horrific Whitechapel murders behind their prison walls. How could they overlook a suspect? How could they not figure out who this person was? That is when an idea hit me. I began to leave little notes for the police. The first was a simple postcard in which I assumed the pseudonym "Saucy Jack." The next came on October 16, 1888 when I sent the famous "From Hell" letter to the head of the Whitechapel Vigilance Committee, enclosed with a human kidney. If that would not scare the rats of Whitechapel, then I knew not what else I could.

By the beginning of November, Garnet was starting to feel hopeless. She had met and been with many men and women, but none seem to suit her interests as a potential progeny. She felt as if they would be too dull to try and train properly in the vampiric ways. One night, after rising from her slumber, she came to my chambers, sitting at the table across from me. This was not the Garnet I was used to seeing. Her gray eyes seemed haunted, and her hair, usually voluminous hung low like dead flowers. She did not look well. She looked ill.

"Garnet, what is it that troubles you?" I asked

concerned.

"My darling one, it is with a heavy bosom that I come to tell you that I wish to return to Romania," she replied softly.

"Are you feeling homesick, my pet?"

"Do you think less of me for admitting that?"

"Never, my lovely one. I, too, am stirring for the familiarity of the Transylvanian countryside. As long as I am alive, I will only ever feel as that is my true home, no matter where it is I stray to. I hope that when you take on your own progeny, that you will remember that Transylvania is your home too."

"I shall always remember my place in your court, Vlad." she choked out as bloody tears creased from their ducts.

I stood and crossed to her side taking her into my arms. I stroked her hair lovingly as I ran my tongue across the blood streaking down her cheek. She trembled a bit as her eyes closed clinging to me like any child to their parent.

"You must know," she began. "My love for you shall always be the greatest. You saved me from inevitable demise."

I thought back to the night in which she became my progeny. She had obtained the consumption and was dying before my eyes. I could not allow myself to let such a precious creature die so young. I had not felt that kind of desire since my late wife threw herself from the palace balcony during the Turkish war. I was lonely, and I pitied this poor child. For the first time in my long life, I wanted to save something rather than destroy it. As such, at the moment, I too felt as if I needed to save Garnet from the heartache of homesickness.

"I will send Crispin out on the morrow to find proper transport home. Until the procurement, you must be patient. However, I believe we should give these fools at the great Scotland Yard one last thrill from ol' Jack."

I watched as Garnet's eyes went from heavy to light. A smile crossed her lips as she touched my chest, fingering my dragon medallion—a symbol of the Order of my family.

"I think you are right, my lord."

Our last victim was a woman named Mary Kelly. Crispin had seen her around during his time in the area. He believed that she liked him because he was not a native Londoner. She had liked his Italian accent and the stripe of gray in his hair that gave him a "scholarly look."

"I am afraid that I am to depart London for my homeland soon," Crispin said to her on the evening of November 8th.

"Oh, please don't go," she pleaded with him.

"I must. I have business to attend to at home. I have been abroad for so long…"

"Then come to me tomorrow night," Kelly said, "I shall give you a going away present that you shall never forget."

Oh that poor Mary Kelly. Poor love struck

Mary Kelly. She never saw her murder coming. That night when he went to her, Crispin drugged the wine he gave to her and we set to work. Mary Kelly went from a somewhat handsome prostitute to having her features hacked away, her body eviscerated, and Crispin, literally, stealing her heart as a souvenir. To this day, I still had never asked his motives in taking her heart. Nonetheless, he brought it back to Romania with us and keeps it in a jar in a chemical preservative.

It has now been four years since the five murders committed in Whitechapel took place. There are many speculations as to the identity of the man the papers have dubbed “Jack the Ripper.” None would ever suspect that he was also known to others as “the Impaler.” Garnet has still not taken a progeny. I fear she is being too picky in her choice. But, I suppose when you are to be stuck with them for at least one hundred and fifty years or more, one must be sure. Crispin is still with us. Currently he is out running in the forests of our village. During a full moon we let him roam free. Also, we are expecting a visitor from London. I wish to procure a property in London to use as a safe house for my children. This young man’s name is Jonathan Harker….

Epilogue

The carriage driver was reluctant to bring the young foreigner out on such a night as this. One did not wander into the forests on Walpurgis Night. But this young Englishman insisted he had a meeting at a nearby castle and he was expected. As the carriage drove in the direction of the castle, a wolf was heard off in the distant tree line.

"How queer," thought the Englishman.

Suddenly, the carriage lurched to a halt, sending the Englishman forward. He heard the cries of the driver and quickly opened the carriage door coming face to face with a blue eyed gray wolf. The young man quickly jumped back into the carriage. There, he picked up his briefcase, deciding it was the best shield he could muster. He got out to the sharp snarls of the wolf. The wolf lunged and tore at the leather case, sending the man stumbling back across a log, tearing a trouser leg in the process. The wolf came closer staring down the man. He did not bite, but blood was crusting around his jowls. The wolf regarded the stranger for a moment before turning and walking off in the direction the carriage had been heading. The man lay on the forest floor, clutching his case to his chest, thanking God to be alive. When he got to his feet, he saw that the driver had been mauled to death by the lone wolf. Knowing he was expected, he took one of the horses and rode in the direction of the castle. He spotted the wolf off in the distance. It was as if this wolf knew exactly where to lead this man. It was nearing sunrise as the man arrived at the castle. Coming from London, this castle was no marvel such as the palaces he had seen line the countryside. He dismounted the borrowed horse and approached the fortified doors, knocking with an over-sized knocker. A dragon's visage held the ring in its mouth. The doors swung open to reveal a beautifully decorated foyer. It was as grand as any dowager house in England.

A man in flowing robes came down the stairs. His black hair reached his shoulders bouncing along as he walked.

"Ah, you must be Mr. Harker, from London, correct?" he asked.

"Yes, sir, and you must be Lord…"

"Count," he corrected the young man. "You may call me Count Dracula."

"Tis a pleasure, Count." Harker offered his hand to shake.

The Count took it slowly and shook. Harker tried not to recoil at the temperature of the Count's hand.

"Forgive my cold hands," he said, sensing Harker's discomfort, "these old castles are a bit drafty. I am afraid it is a bit late to conduct business tonight. Shall we meet for dinner tomorrow evening when we may discuss the property and all of the parameters? I shall also introduce you to my children."

"Oh, you did not mention you were a father, Count," Harker replied a bit confused.

"You could say that," the Count sneered leading Harker to a guest chamber.

The next evening, Jonathan Harker was dressed

in evening attire as he came down to meet with the Count and his family. The Count sat at the head of the table and rose when Harker entered the room. To the left was a brown haired young man with a hint of silver in his hair, to his right a beautiful young woman with a fair complexion and auburn hair that complimented her gray eyes.

"Allow me to introduce my children, Mr. Harker. This is Crispin and Garnet."

"How do you do?" replied Harker, his eyes lingering a moment too long on the woman called Garnet.

"Shall we?" asked the Count motioning to the table.

The meal was quiet and a bit queer to Jonathan Harker. The boy called Crispin ate greedy amounts of meat yet the other two did not seem to do much aside from sip wine from a glass.

"So, did they ever find that Jack the Ripper fellow that was slicing up those women in London?" the Count asked from seemingly nowhere.

"Uh, no," Harker replied, a bit confused at the turn of conversation, "I believe he is still on the lam."

"Pity," said the Count, "Do forgive me, but I am feeling under the weather tonight. I shall leave you in the company of Garnet. Come Crispin."

The men rose from the table leaving the room. As they started up the stairs, they heard Jonathan Harker shriek from the dining hall.

"It seems that our Garnet has found her progeny. An exotic Brit. What hypocrisy is this? And they gave Romani a bad name."

"Perhaps Harker will change her mind?" offered Crispin.

"Perhaps…" mused the Count, "Be kind to your new brother."

THE NEW ALBINO RACE

BY: DONALD ARMFIELD

Zagros Mountains,
Iranian border
Tuesday 1:37 PM

The consolidated mudstone has made the trek up to the highest peak, long and torturous. The temperature drop and the roaring winds rolling down from the mountain tops, makes visibility almost impossible. The atrocious terrain became tiring for the three brothers, but they continued to belt it out knowing the cave they were looking for is up ahead.

The cave dated back to the eighteenth century, B.C. Also said to originally house the "Burney Relief" aka "The Queen of the Night." A clay plaque over a foot tall representing Ishtar, the Sumerian goddess of fertility, love, war and sex. Little is known about it's maker but the supposedly original plaque is displayed in a British Museum. The naked women standing upon two lions with talons of a bird, flanked by owls, is such beauty showing the skills of the ancestors of the Mesopotamian era. The brothers received a valuable tip from a professor back in the states. *"What if more is to be found in that cave?"*

Jarrod, Jordan and Jackson Linderman are numismatics, or coin collectors. Their previous exploring has made them rather popular with museums around the world. Some of their coin collection, dating back to the early Renaissance. If there is a handful of currency or even some kind of token lying in this cave, it may be one of the oldest forms of currency to date for their collection.

"There she is boys," Jordan, the oldest of the brothers says. Jarrod and Jackson stop directly behind Jordan and marvel at the finding of the said cave.

"If we don't find any coins in this cave, I hope there is something that we can return with, after this long freaking cold trip." Jarrod finishes his rant and takes a swig from his water canteen.

"Lets hope so," Jordan says. "Once we get inside the cave it may be a little warmer, I mean at least the frigid wind won't be nipping at our faces."

The entrance of the cave is just tall enough for all the Linderman brothers to pass over the threshold without ducking. They stop just a few steps in. Jackson pulls a cone shaped torch holder out of his backpack, with large round wick attached to the top. He spins the dial of his zippo and the torch comes to life. "Let there be light," Jackson tosses out the corny comment. Jackson hangs a cigarette from his lip and uses the torch to light it.

"Any idea how deep this cave runs?" Jarrod asks.

"I'm going to flip on our trusty device to track our miles. Looking ahead it looks as though the cave has a steep downslope," Jordan continues, "If breathing starts to cut short we may need to pull out our breathing equipment."

"You know what bro," Jarrod starts speaking with the cigarette hanging from his lip. "I did a little further research on these mountains. According to what I found these here caves may have been inhabited by Babylonian tribes, who invaded the Sumerian peoples of Mesopotamia."

"Sweet, maybe we will find some skulls of the dead Mesopotamian people." Jackson says.

"Let's keep moving," Jordan says, pulling his hood back. "And pay attention to your breathing as we get deeper into this cave. By the way we are looking for an altar of some type if my studies are correct."

The Linderman brothers grew up in a modest home on the western border of Massachusetts. Their mother ran a sewing company out of their home. She made women belts with tacky looking belt buckles and every Easter and Christmas, she made dresses for their cousins. The Linderman's father was always on an exploration traveling to other countries. Well, that is what their mother told them. They actually have short memories of their father and occasionally received Christmas or Birthday cards on the wrong dates.

When Jordan, the oldest brother, turned sixteen he went to a local restaurant in search of a job. He scored a job as a busboy and enjoyed his job and saved pretty much every penny he made. His other two brothers followed in his footsteps when they turned sixteen. Jarrod worked at a car wash station and Jackson dressed up in different cartoon characters, on the weekends at The Birthday Zone Place.

As years went by their mother started showing signs of cancer and passed away. The brothers were devastated, but kept their chins high and carried on to pursue their dreams. They sold the home they grew up in and moved into a loft styled apartment closer to the city. After four months of living together, Jordan came across an old tattered map with some kind of buried treasure that was supposedly never claimed. The brothers took the map serious and found a large chest of coins from the early 18th century. Noticing all the money that museums were willing to pay for such things, they decided to continue this life style and find more.

"Bro, I don't believe we can go any further." Jackson says, holding the torch, looking down over a cliffs edge.

"Do you think our treasure is down there?" Jordan asks, spitting over the edge of the dead end.

"Rope me in, Bro." Jarrod says, getting Jordan's attention. Jarrod drops his backpack onto the ground and begins pulling out the ropes and hooks.

Jordan hammers one of the hooks into the chasm and feeds some of the rope through, looping a bowline knot with two turns of the rope. He gives the knot three quick tugs and says, "Ready to go,

Jarrod."

"Whose got that hand held spotlight?" Jarrod asks.

"I got it in my backpack," Jackson yells out in response. Jackson pulls out the hand held spotlight, flicks the switch on and passes it to his brother. Jarrod adjusts his footing over the edge of the hole and says, "Here goes the neighborhood, boys."

"Be careful, Bro," Jackson and Jordan say, in unison with each other.

Jarrod takes three quick inhale/exhales and jumps back, sliding down the first foot into the dark hole. He continues the descent with ease jumping back and fourth from side to side, down the darkened aperture, stopping in between each slide and shining the spotlight below his feet. Another slide on the rope and he touches ground level. "Hey guys, my feet are planted," Jarrod yells up to his brothers. He shines the spotlight upwards to the top of the aperture. Jordan yells down to him, "What do you see little bro?"

"It looks like a path leading down another dark corridor. Maybe one of you should come down here so we can loop in a safety rope to follow me."

"Okay bro, I'll be right down," Jackson yells down the hole to his brother. Jackson latches in to the same hook Jarrod used to descend into the dark hole. He adjusts his gloves and throws an extra coil of rope over his shoulder. Giving Jordan a head nod, he begins to slide down the chasm's dead end hole.

Jackson hits the bottom with an abrupt landing, his ankle snaps under his weight. “Awe shit!” he yells.

“Are you alright?” Jarrod asks.

“Yeah, I'm good just twisted my ankle a little.”

Jarrod shines the spotlight in Jackson's direction and watches him limp a little over to the wall. Jackson pulls a hook he affixed to his belt loop and holds it against the chasm wall. He grabs the hammer from the back of his pants and hammers the hook into the wall. Loops the extra rope through the eye hook and flips another bowline knot. “Ready to go, man?” Jackson says. Jarrod unlatches his line he used to descend with and hooks on to the new line. A fist bump exchange with his brother and he heads off down the darkened corridor, shining the spotlight up ahead.

Jarrod feels a damp breeze brush over him. He shakes it off and continues to walk slow and steady down the corridor. Within a few more steps he crosses over into a larger area in height compared to the corridor he just traveled. Standing before him is a three-step altar, with a pedestal made of stone sitting in the center. “I found the altar,” Jarrod yells, his voice echoes off the corridor walls.

Jackson limps fast, cringing with each step with torn ankle through the corridor with a smaller flashlight in hand. “Yo Jordan, get a new line in and get your ass down here, you've got to see this,” Jackson yells over his shoulder.

Jordan wastes no time and ropes in on the same hook his brother hooked into. With haste and ease he slides down the hole to the bottom. Unlatching his line, he pulls a flashlight out of a little nap sack attached to his belt loop. Running down the corridor to catch up to his brothers, Jordan stops beside his brothers and stares at the altar. Jordan gets closer, stepping on the first of three steps.

A deep blue lapis lazuli rock in the shape of a flute rests upon the pedestal in the center of the altar. Jordan climbs the remaining two steps, being aware of his surroundings with each step. He reaches out and touches the ancient flute.

"Jordan, be careful," Jarrod says. "Between all those Indiana Jones movies and Tomb Raider games I'm sure there is some type of trap door or something over there."

"Only in the movies," Jordan says and lifts the flute off the pedestal. He pauses for a dramatic effect, but nothing happens. Holding the flute, Jordan turns to look at his brothers. Jarrod lets out a loud fart, "Sorry I had to. The dead silence was killing me."

"No coins, but look at this," Jordan says, holding the blue flute in the spotlight.

"Let's get out of this cavern before it starts to crumble," Jarrod says.

The Linderman brothers get out of the cavern with no sudden crumbling effect, chasing behind them. They check their equipment at the threshold of the exit. Jordan puts the blue-stone flute under his arm and adjusts the zipper on his coat. A frigid wind gust blows into the mouth of the cave. "God-dammit, that is cold," Jackson yells, turning his back to the wind. Jordan turns to his side as he continues to tighten up his jacket.

The freezing wind brushes over the tip of the flute. A melodious chime plays into the open air. The terrain around the entrance to the cave begins to shake. An abundant amount of snow and rock comes thundering down from the peak of the mountain. "I knew this was going to happen," Jackson yells out, looking up and over the cave entrance, with the snow almost gliding over his head. The large amount of snow and rock lands on the open path below—the same path the brothers followed to reach the cave.

"Watch Out!" Jarrod yells out, before finishing the last word he grabs hold of Jackson. Jumping backwards and landing just under the threshold of the cave a huge piece of rubble blocks the entrance. "This is going to suck, bros." Jackson continues, "Just like the movie "*Alive*" we will be eating each other, real soon."

"Lets stay calm," Jordan says. "We have instincts, lets put our heads together and figure this out."

"What's that noise?" Jarrod cuts in, "You hear it?"

The sound of burrowing from below sounds

more like a distant static. Jarrod and Jordan are standing completely still, feeling the damp dirt around their feet begin to soften up. Jackson looks as though he is sinking into the dirt. "Guys, what the hell is happening?" Jackson says, reaching out to his sides trying to grasp onto something.

A creature with broad shoulders and a cone-shaped head pops up and out of the dirt. It's long dangling, tentacle-fingers looking like some kind of lobster claw, clamps down over Jackson's head. Jackson goes to yell out something, but quickly takes a deep breath as he disappears in the dirt.

Two more of the creatures with the oddly shaped heads peek their heads out of the dirt. Jarrod and Jordan go to run, but quickly begin to sink into the ripples of dirt created by the strange creatures. One of the creatures makes some kind of high pitch bellow noise and reaches out towards Jordan. Jordan puts up a useless struggle with the creature's strong grip pulling him under, into the sinking dirt underground.

Somewhere Underground
Zagros Mountains,
Wednesday 8:32 AM

"Psst!" Jarrod makes a noise to get one of his

brothers attention, who is also tied up to a rock post like his self. Jordan picks his head up from its awkward resting position on his shoulder.

"I feel like I've been drugged," he says while snapping out of his long unexpected deep sleep. "And I'm still hearing noises. Sounds like someone is shuffling their feet over the dirt."

"Shhh!" Jordan quickly says, "Pretend we're still sleeping."

A male figure with a long maroon robe enters the small room. A necklace hangs from around his neck, a medallion of intertwining snakes. He moves as if he is floating. With two of the large mole looking creatures dragging their feet behind him. The man's face lacks any pigmentation of color, including his long hair resting on his shoulders in a pure white. He stops in the middle of the room and begins to rub his hands together. "Get me the taller one, over there," the man says to the mole creature to his right. The mole creature has trouble walking, dragging it's feet with sluggish movements, almost looking like its a struggle to walk. "Quicker, Scum!" The man yells, sheathing a bullwhip from a loop on his robe. He cracks the bullwhip catching the sluggish mole creature in the back of the neck. The creature lets out a bellow, but continues to move at the same speed.

The creature's tentacle-fingers work faster than it's legs, removing the ropes from Jarrod's wrist. Still bound at the feet Jarrod tries to take a few swings with his fist at the mole man, but falls to the ground. The other mole man grabs Jarrod by the feet and starts to drag him along the ground. “Let me go, you ugly piece of shit!” Jarrod yells.

“What the fuck are you going to do with us?” Jordan asks.

“You will all get a turn soon, just hang out for a few.” The albino looking man says, laughing with a snort at his lame joke.

Jarrod comes walking back in to the small room, where his brothers are still bound to stone posts. Following behind him is a beautiful woman, with wavy red hair and a nice meaty shape to her body. Her long dress has a solo horizontal strap over her left shoulder. She is bare foot and looks transfixed deep in her thoughts.

The lady reties Jarrod's wrist to the post and spins on heel to leave. “Hey, you let them treat you like that?” Jordan asks the woman, noticing the whipping marks on her back, through the opening in her dress.

“Excuse me!” The woman replies.

“You let them whip you like that?” Jordan redirects the question.

The redheaded woman drops her head and looks at the ground on her way out of the room. She says, “I'll be back soon with some rations,” disappearing under the small archway of the room.

“We need to get out of here guys,” Jarrod says, tugging a little with the bounding around his wrist. “Those mole creatures have different species. Well, one struck me with a needle and drew blood from me, it looked almost human besides his face.” Jarrod continues to struggle with the ropes around his wrist. “It smells like rotting flesh going down the corridor on the way back here and beside the beautiful red hair who guided me I think we are the only other actual humans.”

“Hell yeah!” Jackson yells out, “I'm free! Time to get the fuck out of here.”

Jackson takes a few side steps and quickly unties Jordan from his post. Then runs across the center of the small room to Jarrod and unties him. “Now what?” Jordan says, rubbing his wrist from the chafing of the rope.

“Shit! I hear someone coming. Lets just look like we are still tied up, quick guys.” Jackson says and hustles back on over to his post. Jarrod and Jordan follow his lead and run back to their posts.

A different redheaded woman walks into the room with a serving tray. Three of the mole creatures come in directly behind her, dragging a wooden table and some chairs. Two of the mole creatures set up the wooden table, while the remaining one places the chairs around the table. They turn and exit the room leaving just the redhead standing with the tray still in her arms.

The woman places the tray on the wooden table and says, "Y'all get to eat now, but you must corporate and let me tie you to the chairs." She walks up to Jordan and reaches for his wrist. Jordan spins the redhead around with his left arm and puts his right hand over her mouth.

"Shhh! I won't hurt you. Just help us get out of here," Jordan says.

"I can't help you. He will let my flesh scorch and mutilate in the blinding light," the redheaded woman says.

"We will put an end to him. Are you talking about that man in the robe with the pail skin?" Jordan turns the woman around and looks into her eyes.

"Yes, he calls himself, Tammuz. The harvester of an albino race of the dead. I've escorted many of the fallen to the dark chambers behind these halls. These mole people are his slaves, his hunters to climb to the surface and collect his victims. I've watch many suffer unwilling to a martyr of cruel rituals dropped in the chambers. Ones who fail to meet an ordinance to his liking is brought to the light."

"This is heavy," Jackson says.

"May I ask your name, hun?" Jordan asks the

redheaded woman.

"My name is Star. I am the last of the women ancestors of *the early dynastic period.* My five brothers sunk into a siphoning sand funnel one day out in the field. I listened to their screams for help, that fell to deaf ears. I jumped into the sand funnel right before it closed up, in hopes to save them. Tammuz quickly made me his sexual desire and my brothers became the firsts of his albino race."

"Star, sorry I don't mean to cut you off, but I plan on escaping this hell hole and if I have to I'll take you with me and any other humans in here with you."

"We don't have much time. Your brothers chromosomes was injected into the stratosphere dwelling of the albino race. Soon more will harvest and bloom into new death. From what I understand, the next injection will be the last and the expectant of the new race. It will rise to the living world, and your brother was that next injection."

"Well, lets get rambling. Where does this ugly transparent fucker hideout?" Jordan inquires, rubbing his hands together with excitement.

"I will guide you, but I will not fight by your side. I'm afraid of Tammuz's powers. I've seen them first hand, you must be careful. Come follow me." Star says, turning towards the archway and exiting into the corridor.

"I will bring up the dead to eat the living.
And the dead will outnumber the living."

Somewhere Underground Zagros Mountains, Wednesday 5:36 PM

The corridor did indeed reek of dead things, decaying flesh, or unwashed bodies. The Linderman brothers walk down the many, twisting corridors, narrowly lit by torches along the walls. Jackson's ankle has began to feel a little better, as Star pretty much lead the way. At the end of one of the many corridors the brothers and Star stop in front of a door. The door has a label on it that reads, *"Harvesting Room."*

"My brothers must remember me, after all these years," Star continues, as she pulls the latch connected to the door. "No matter the living torture they endured." At the last word Star pushes open the door and it swings open with ease.

The other side of the door reveals a garden patch with nothing but mounds of dirt, housing the bodies of humans---with just their heads showing out the tops of the collected dirt mounds. Directly in the center of the garden, sits a throne looking structure entwined with drab, twisting roots. The pale-colored man, known as Tammuz has long tubes protruding out of his body. His arms and legs look as if they are throbbing from the inside, with liquid consumption.

"What the fuck is going on, Star?" Jordan says out loud.

"I've opened this door many times before, you must speak quietly when Tammuz is in his photosynthesis process," Star says, in a low whisper. "I believe my brothers are still buried in one of these mounds, please help me find them."

"Is he seriously sucking the life out of these people?" Jackson says, with a smirk on his face. "This is fucking awesome!" Jackson's excitement came out a little too loud.

Suddenly a loud hissing noise echoes throughout the entire garden-room, like a steam powered engine releasing an excess build up. The tubes penetrating Tammuz fall out the punctured holes along his body. Tammuz opens his eyes and speaks in a dull roar, "I must lash out and disembowel the being who interferes with my transpiration." He slowly opens his eyes.

"This is going to get ugly. Isn't it?" Jarrod says, slowly turning and walking down between two of the garden patches.

"I'm with you, bro," Jackson says. "Oh, tiptoe through the garden and tiptoe through the tulips with me," Jackson continues to sing in a quiet tone walking down the same path as his brother.

Jordan is walking ahead on an adjacent path through the large garden-room. Star is beside him running along on her hands and knees, pulling dirt away from the drained human beings. Their eyes look transfixed, staring off into another dimension. Most of their pigmentation is gone, only small amounts of flesh color still showing on their faces. Some of the humans almost look transparent, as if you can see their insides working, to keep them alive.

Star pauses in front of a body. She grabs hold of the chin of a male figure and looks him dead in the eyes. Star lets out a whimper and squeezes a pile of the moist dirt in her hand. She stands up from the ground and drops the dirt out of her hand, takes a deep breath and yells, "I will kill you, Tammuz."

Tammuz looks fully rejuvenated from his photosynthesis process and begins to glow---as he rises up from the ground he says, "I gave you eternal life as a servant. A servant for the king of the new race that will outnumber the living."

"You killed my brothers," Star yells.

"I sacrificed their souls, in exchange for a warrior of the New Race. He will battle the humans, until they bow to me and become part of the ancient race, or parish before me." Tammuz replies.

"You will do no such thing," Jordan cuts in.

"You imbeciles are no match for me," Tammuz says. "I won't even waste my time to smite thee with my own hands. GUARDS, CEASE THESE GRUBS IN MY GARDEN!"

Conical shaped mounds of dirt replies to the demand, in a spiraling locomotion action. Passing directly under the footing of Star and the Linderman brothers. Blasting dirt clots into the air five bulky mole creatures appear. The mole creatures take a stance in a fighting pose and look at it's assailants as pest.

Jordan takes a quick glance over at Tammuz, who escapes under a small passageway on the other side of the garden. The mole creatures begin making disgruntle, mumbling noises and moving in closer ready to attack. "What are we doing guys?" Jarrod yells out, taking steps backwards and keeping his sight on the mole creatures.

"I say we fight these filthy rats, and bury them dead," Jackson says, interlocking his fingers and cracking them. "What do you say, Jordan?"

"I'm with ya, bro. Let's kill these fuckers!"

Suddenly the arms and legs of the mole creature start to bulge and pulsate. The torn and tattered cloth used as a garment of clothing to cover the creatures, rips down the center of its chest. They hold their arms up in the air and let out a booming roar, that shakes the ceiling of the garden-room. The mole creatures grow in size and within seconds, begin stomping through the soil with so much fierce.

Two of the creatures head in Jarrod's direction, who is showing the most fear.

"Jarrod, RUN!" Jordan yells. Jarrod turns quickly on his heel and hurtles over the dirt hedges, heading to the other side of the garden-room.

"Hey, boys," Star shouts out, from the small entrance where Tammuz escaped. "Need some swords?" Star tosses three broadswords from the entrance. The swords soar through the air and stick in the soil. Jordan shrugs at the sudden turn of events, runs over to one of the broadswords and pulls it out of the soil.

Jordan turns around just in time to see one of the beastly moles, stomping behind him. He holds the sword tight and snaps his arm out stiff, at the same moment the mole-beast reaches out for him---catching the broadsword in the creature's eye cavity. The creature lets out a bellowing cry, throwing his arms out to its side. The mole-beast grabs the blade of the sword and tears it out of his eye socket. Blood pouring out of it's eye socket, torn flesh collected on the sword. It does not seem to put a damper on his approach and it's reach to grab the brother. Jordan runs for the sword this time with a forward roll. Grabbing hold of the sword, Jordan jumps and glides in mid-air for a few moments. Coming down in front of the mole-beast, driving the sword in the gullet of it's neck. The beastly creature gurgles and grabs hold of the blade, while falling forward, landing in an upright position on the swords handle. The creature's dying moments show in it's eyes, as the blade protrudes and pops out the back of it's neck.

"Bro, that was fucking awesome," Jackson shows his excitement. "Now, watch me."

Jackson shows off with a series of tumbling acrobats across the soil. He grabs one of the other broadswords from the ground and starts swinging it in the air. The momentum picks him up off the ground. Jackson looks like a helicopter hovering over head, a blast of light barrels him forward in the direction of one of the other mole-beast. With two swift slices in the shape of an X, the creature's brawn upper body slumps on to the ground, like a sliding jigsaw puzzle, the legs still standing erect.

One of the remaining mole-beast comes running, in large struts. “How bout a melon on a stick!” Jackson says, throwing his broadsword into the air. The sword penetrates through the creature's skull and without another running step, it crashes into the soil face first. The blood of the creature pours out, quickly forming a puddle around it's head, lying dead on the ground.

The last two mole seem dumbstruck, but still having a fierce look and ready to attack. Jordan walks up to the the mole-beast he slayed and steps on the creature's head. He grasps the handle of the sword lodged in the creature's neck and rips it out. The two remaining creatures start convulsing and twitching, their skin bubbling with blisters through the fur on their backs. Black fluid starts to pour out of their snouts. The blisters on their backs raise in increasing amounts, covering the creature's legs and arms. Growing in size, the blisters begin to burst. The black plasma-like fluid discharging from their broken skin. The mole-beast pause for a second with no physical movements, their bodies bulge like a balloon, then bursts.

The black liquid, blood and body innards of the creatures, splatter around the garden-room. Their pelts, still connected to a layer of skin lying in a heaping mess in the soil. Pieces of mole-beast viscera clings to Jackson's clothing. He looks over at Jarrod who is hunched over, holding his head. Jackson and Jordan both walk up to Jarrod and reach out to tap him on the shoulder, to reassure him of the ending. Jarrod shoots up from his hunched over form and yells, “Is it over?”

Jarrod's face is a pale-white color, like the pigmentation was sucked out of him. The veins in his face show more visibly, but his veins are green. A mapping display of flowing blood, dyed green. His fingers have small leaf pedals growing out the tips of them.

“What the fuck is wrong with you, bro?” Jordan says.

Jarrod holds his hands out and looks at them, noticing his green veins and leaflets poking out his fingertips. “What the hell is happening to me? It's that shit they injected in me.”

Star comes into the room riding some kind of round terracotta saucer. The soundless saucer carrying Star stops in the center of the garden-room. Star tilts her head back and opens her mouth. A green mist shoots out of her mouth, and quickly covers the entire room. After a brief pause, Star begins to speak, "Thou has fell into our trap. The blood of man will tarnish the garden and bring forth the new race."

"Star, I thought you were going to help us?" Jordan cuts in.

"You brothers have such handsome features that I love. I have brought you here to my garden of lies and lost. You three will be the last, finally to bring my everlasting love back from dead."

"What the fuck are you talking about?" Jordan yells out.

"Man of the current century are easily fooled. As you can see many have perished before my act of save the beautiful girl. I needed the souls of many men to harvest in Tammuz's garden. He will now be able to rise from the underworld with me and carry out the new race."

"Fuck you, we will be doing nothing for your garden," Jordan says, while trying to move and noticing his feet sinking in the soil. A vine wraps around his legs and holds him upright.

Jordan looks over at Jackson, seeing that he is also covered in vines. Jarrod has went back to his hunched over frightening form, rocking back and forth. The vines grab hold of Jarrod and snap him to an erect stance, lowering his feet into the soil.

"At last the three remaining souls are in place, blood has spread over the garden and together my love Tammuz, and myself can live in the living world once again," Star continues to chant. "play ye for me, ye weepers and lamenting women! That the dead may rise up and inhale the incense."

Hearing the chant and the word 'play' gave Jordan a thought. He remembers the flute in the cargo pocket of his jeans. With the vines wrapped tightly around his legs, he knew he wasn't going to get hold of the flute. He tightens his leg muscle and feels the old wooden flute buckle against his leg. Suddenly the vines constricting him and his brother come loose and drop them to the soil.

Star continues to chant, "play ye for me, ye weepers and lamenting women! That the dead may rise up and inhale the incense."

"Hey bitch! In case you haven't noticed your precious treasure is in my possession." Jordan yells out, holding the now broken flute in the air.

Star stops her chant and looks over at Jordan. She begins to notice all her collected bodies deteriorating to skeletons. What-ever was holding the life in all those suffered people finally laid to rest. The soil covering the ground in the garden-room, begins to harden, losing its moist texture. Overhead a ghostly figure stops just above Star's head. The ghostly figure is Tammuz holding his hand out to touch Star one last time and then fades out into the air.

"What have you done?" Star falls to her knees and cries.

The Linderman brothers re-group in the center of the fallen garden-room. Jarrod has returned to normal, no longer looking like the stem of a plant. Jordan steps up to Star and says, "Direct us out of this poor, pathetic hope of a new race, shithole. Now!"

"I will have my race outnumber the living one day. Tammuz will be my lover and we will dance over our new world together."

"Whatever bitch, get us out of this mountain and you can do just that," Jordan replies, forcefully grabbing her by the arm."

A blast of light returns the brothers to the base of the mountain. Coats fully zipped and gear strapped to their backs, as if it was two days ago when they first climbed the mountain.

"Can you say, deja vu," Jackson says.

"Yeah, I feel that too, but yet I still have this." Jordan holds up the broken flute.

A hint of quiet tone plays off the top of the broken flute. A flurry of snow, casting off the mountain caps from above, swirls through the clouds. The Linderman brothers look at each other and wonder if Star was bluffing, about her new race outnumbering the living one day.

THE CREATURE RIDES AMONG US

BY: KEVIN CANDELA

The Cast:
May Jean – Owner of The Riptide Oceanside Tavern

The Chargers:
Brentley Hosslan
Zeke Obert
Fred Stossi
Sharla Mills
Gilbert (Gibby) Mann Landers (Simon Tallin)

The Marauders:
Aggie Tools
Chita Velez
Clyde Northway
Jeri Wells
Lou Bender
Mac Learing

"Those Black Lagoon movies were fiction. They weren't based on nothin' other than some writer's imagination in the wee dim hours of the 1950s."

"Oh, come on Zeke. You watch them shows about monster huntin' and after a while you start to think that hey, if there's a Lizard Man in North Carolina and a Mantis Man in New Jersey then who knows what they might find way up some prehistoric river like the…"

"I don't watch 'em, and there ain't none of neither!"

"Technically, Scape Ore Swamp is in South Carolina, Fred."

"*South.* Right. Sorry, May Jean. You watch 'em too, huh?"

The seen-it-all tavern owner just smiled and kept drying permanently spotty bar glasses.

"She probably just knows geography," Zeke

said. "Ain't nothin' superstitious about that." He slugged down the last of his Guinness and belched. "And forget that garbage about real life men-fish. That video was just as made up as any other one. It's the Age of the Hoax."

"I saw that," Sharla Mills said. "If you ask me," she went on, nodding at the leather-clad hulk effectively occupying the next two bar stools to her left, "the guy in the video looked just like old Landers here."

The immense man seated at her left elbow just grunted and grinned.

"Oh, come on," Zeke said as the rest of the gang – and May Jean – chuckled. "That video is shot from so far away all you can tell is that the guy is…uh …"

With Landers' almost black eyes on him Zeke wasn't sure how to finish.

"That word you're looking for," Sharla said, enjoying the moment, "how about robust?"

Landers was still just glaring.

"I swear Zeke," May Jean said. "You oughta take a lesson from The Quiet Man there."

Fred laughed. Landers shrugged it off and went back to his drink.

The tension was gone, but not for long. The muffled rumble of bikes signaled its return.

"They're here," Fred said.

"Really?" Sharla shot back. "What was your first clue?"

The big engines went silent. So did the bar. May Jean spoke as the thudding and jingling of numerous boots grew louder beyond the front door.

"Remember, kids," she said, "this is neutral ground, not a play pen for alleged grownups." She locked gazes with Brent Hosslan. "Got that?" she said without a trace of mirth.

"Really, May Jean," Brent said, "you have to ask?"

The front door opened.

Aggie Tools was first in the door, dressed mean-slutty-hot and ready for action.

"Hi Brent," she said cheerfully. "You're looking ugly as usual."

Aggie's five filed in behind her as she went over to where Hosslan was standing, hands on hips. She stopped a few feet short of him and mimed his pose there.

"How's tricks, Brentley?"

"I'm sure I can't keep up with yours, Aggie. But I can't bitch."

"Really? What's changed?"

Her gang had clustered together just inside the door. She spun on them.

"Well," she said, "you need introductions or something? Grab a seat."

Chita and Clyde went over to the bar on the far side of Landers, the only member of Brent's group not to have even bothered to turn from his spot at the bar yet. He didn't even glance their way as they sat down.

May Jean took their orders – Scotch rocks for her, Cuervo for him – while the other three took seats at the table nearest the door.

"Outnumbered again," Brent said.

"Not my fault," Aggie said. "Who's your no-show?"

"Simon had to bail. Sick kid."

"Too bad. He's gonna miss it."

"You're all heart, Aggie."

She shrugged. "We are what we are. You ready to talk?"

"What's to talk?"

"True enough. I suppose we can just get straight to it. Got the cash?"

Brent looked over at the bar.

"Landers?" he said.

Landers turned and rose. He lumbered over toward Aggie and Brent, reaching inside his jacket as he went. He pulled out two big bundles of twenties and held them out for Aggie, who grabbed them up and started flipping through one.

"Gawwwd," she declared, her sharp little features scrunching with revulsion. "These stink!" Moving them well out from under her chin she looked over at Brent. "Why'd you have *him* carry your stake?"

"Would YOU try to take cash off him?"

Aggie looked Landers up and down.

"I might not walk right up to him," she conceded. "And if he smells like this money I wouldn't sneak up on him either. It'd take a month's worth of ketchup baths to get his stank off me."

"I've never noticed anything," Sharla said.

"Of course you haven't, bitch," Aggie said. "You probably smell worse."

Sharla's jaw clenched.

"Easy Shar Baby," Brent said. "She's gonna try to throw us off our game. It's really their only chance to beat us and she knows it."

"Bullshit," Aggie said. "We've got the skills to withstand the thrills and give you and your butt buddies the ills and send you home with chills."

"That's beautiful," Sharla said, "did you work on it all night?"

"Sharla …"

"I'm just fightin' brimstone with fire, Brent."

"And this money smells like the Devil's ass," Aggie said. "If we win you're swapping it out with something that hasn't been in your buddy's armpit."

"I'll take those odds," Brent said, smiling, and he thrust a hand out to her.

She leaned over and sniffed it before finally shaking on the deal.

"Just had to be sure," she said, grinning. "All things considered who knows where *that's* been!"

As agreed upon both teams' stakes – 20 grand each – were left with May Jean at the Riptide Bayside. The eleven competitors-to-be took off together.

he race course was by necessity as far from civilization as it was possible to get. The rugged strip of coastal hills six miles from the Riptide was virtually uninhabited and offered plenty of room, and each year the course was laid out there differently… although always with minimal crossovers of the local roads. To ensure even more privacy for this highly illegal and fairly dangerous run it was started as close to dusk as possible and riders were forbidden to use lights. On most of the newer Harleys the lights came on automatically, so to participate in this rally their owners had to find ways to temporarily disable the light sensor system. Most of the riders were tech savvy enough to do this and the rest – none were hurting for money – could hire someone.

The race always concluded at a secluded beach with an all-nighter so that no one had to drive home with their lights out. The kegs were already chilled there and being watched over by wives, girlfriends…and in Sharla's case her husband Gregg, who didn't ride either, but also didn't have the guts to stand up to his attractive but reckless wife and tell her just how dangerous he really thought it was.

The hills were throwing long shadows by the time the racers were revving up. Ahead of them the uneven shrub-dotted terrain lay striped in rusty sunlight and shade. The breeze was cool, nearly chilling, and steady, and strong enough to be more fairly called wind.

Ten bikes lined up side by side. Aggie tweaked her throttle and her over-sized ride bucked and scooted past them all. She guided it over to about the middle of the pack and then pivoted to face them.

"All right," she hollered, her tinny voice just the right pitch to be heard over all the revving. "You all know the Marble Rally rules. No lights. Our people at the party site are monitoring the police band so if you get reported you're out. And if you see the authorities coming your way you veer off the course, let them catch you and just claim to be on a joyride solo. Keep your phone someplace safe so that if you ditch and get stuck you can call us to come get you…AFTER the race. Main thing is not to get hurt. But if you do then call nine-one-one and again claim you're out here goofing around solo. Might want to say your light got knocked out by the accident too." She glanced over at Brent. "Anything else?" she yelled.

He shrugged and shook his head.

"One more thing," Aggie yelled. "I hope everybody's ditched their colors for this one?"

She looked around and made sure everyone nodded and/or gave the thumbs up.

"Okay now," she said, "getting on time. Let's line 'em up. First Marauder to the…I mean first side to the beer wins!"

She joined the rest. Now eleven were evenly lined up on the crest of the low hill.

She studied her watch.

"A minute to go!" she yelled.

The revving got louder.

"Ten seconds! Nine…eight…"

The engines were virtually drowning her out. She completed the countdown anyway, relying on only those to either side of her – Brent and Mac Learing – as witnesses.

"…two…one…GO!"

The race was on. There was still plenty of light so all eleven shot down the hill, dodging and weaving through the grasses, succulents and shrubs with little trouble.

Trouble would come later when the obstacles – and the ground – got harder to see. This race tended to start in a blitz and end in a crawl. At least until the last few hundred yards on the beach.

The trick with the race was that only one person – this year it was Zeke's on again-off again girlfriend Peg – knew where the dozen route markers had been placed. She'd gone out that morning (for three hundred bucks and an invitation to the kegger) and set the bricks – painted glow-in-the-dark green – at various spots where the racers could see them. Beside each brick she'd set open-topped jars containing a dozen large marbles of the same color: blue at the first stop, for example, and yellow at the second. Every biker was to take and bag a single marble at each stop and then move on. No throwing the jar, spilling it or hiding it was allowed. The penalty was your team forfeiting so generally speaking the jars were to be found where they'd been placed. All the marbles had been indelibly marked with the arbitrary "symbol of authenticity" that Peg had chosen at her whim. This year the mark was an eye, like the one on the top of the dollar bill pyramid.

The winner was the first to arrive at the keg party, but only so long as he or she also had the most marbles. A first place finish was worth 12 points, marbles one point each. Highest cumulative total was the winner. So, it was possible for a first place finisher with only six marbles to lose to a third place finisher with nine, as had in fact happened the previous year with Sharla knocking off an extremely displeased Aggie by one total point…and thus claiming the Chargers' sixth win in the past nine games.

Aggie wasn't patient enough to ever get all twelve. She'd once gotten ten, but finished a dismal eighth out of twelve that year. She tended to overshoot bricks and then get too angry about having to double back for the marbles she'd missed. And take random shortcuts on whims. And be drunk when the game began.

Nobody ever challenged her about it either, at least not since Hal Linneman had a couple of years back and she had responded by summarily dumping him from both her bed and the gang.

Not this year though. This year she was not

only sober (and had been for two days) but determined to get every single marble. And more importantly win. Even more critically she had to be the one to get the win for The Marauders. Herself. She'd never managed it before.

She shot well out ahead on the impetus of two things: the relatively light weight of both herself and her bike and the fact that most of the other riders – male and female alike – couldn't help but want to hold back a little and enjoy the view. Slutty-looking clothing aside (as it often was) she was still an impressively well-built woman, and she had no problem showing off the goods.

Right now the show was doing its job.

Aggie slowed down.

Zeke rumbled up beside her.

"Lookin' good today honey," he hollered, grinning over at her.

Her response was a carefully timed swerve in his direction that made him veer and sent him careening roughly through the middle of a coastal shrub cluster.

"SLUT!" she heard him holler at her back. She grinned.

"Best slut you ever had," she muttered to herself.

She heard a metal growl off to her left. Fellow Marauder Jeri Wells was taking the lead and was too far away to intimidate. Jeri was a newcomer and just a little too fresh-faced and wholesomely appealing for Aggie's tastes anyway. Aggie hadn't even slept with her yet.

Worse yet Jeri had just found the first brick!

Now Aggie had good reason to veer her way, which she did sharply. She cut a couple of others off, including Brent, in her dash to be second to the marker. She arrived just ahead of Brent. Jeri already had her blue marble and was back on her bike and continuing up the hillside.

Aggie was cursing under her breath as she set the bike on its terrain-modified kickstand and hustled over to the former peanut butter jar. She snatched a marble out of it even as Brent was coming up to do the same.

"Tied so far," Brent said.

"Bite me."

"As long as my girlfriend can watch."

He said that last line to her back, for she was already re-mounting her bike.

They hit the non-trail again.

Now both Aggie and Brent were watching Jeri's butt bounce up and down hillsides ahead of them. She had at least a fifty yard lead on them.

Aggie was so worried about the widening gap that she rode right past the second brick. Her clue that this had happened came as she caught Brent breaking her way and then dropping back behind her. She spotted him over her shoulder.

"Damn it!"

She wheeled her bike around. Brent was already off his and taunting her with his yellow marble. He actually let her pull up.

"Gimme one!"

He smiled and slowly extended the jar toward her. But as she reached out he knelt and set it back down near the brick.

"Jackass!"

"I love you too babe."

Brent jumped back on his bike and rode off relishing Aggie's curses.

Jeri pulled up.

"That was kind of nasty," she told Aggie.

"What do you expect?" Aggie shot back. "He's an idiot. And he's the best one they've got." She saw that Jeri had moved in close and was kind of hinting at being handed a marble so she didn't have to get off her ride, but there was no way. "Well, gotta stay on his sorry ass," Aggie said, and she set the jar back down and hustled back over to her bike. "See ya at the finish line."

Jeri watched her ride away, shaking her head.

"Bitch," she muttered.

True to the way most of these rides had gone the leaders went off track. Brent strayed inland a bit and Aggie stayed right on his tail. Jeri had nearly caught up with them when she happened to glance back over her shoulder and notice that the rest weren't following them. Scanning to her left then she soon spotted Landers' huge silhouette as he reached the crest of a low hill atop his gigantic Hog.

He sank from sight behind that hilltop as Aggie watched.

"Damn it!" she said, and turned sharply his way.

Sure enough Sharla, Clyde and Mac Learing were all passing around a marble jar at the base on the far side of the hill. Landers was pulling up there too now. Jeri hit it and shot down the hill.

Clyde and Mac were off and searching again by the time Jeri arrived.

"Hi Shar," Jeri said. "Feeling charitable?"

"You mean am I gonna be an ass like Aggie and set the marble jar back down?"

She acted like she was going to do just that, but instead she tossed a marble to Jeri.

Mac laughed. He hit the throttle and spun out, slinging gravel that sprayed Jeri's chaps.

Landers scowled. "Hey, how about me?" he grumbled in that ocean-deep voice.

"Can't you just lean down from your bike and pick 'em up yourself, stud?" Sharla said, but she grinned and tossed him one anyway.

He missed it.

"Butterpaw," Sharla said with a chuckle. "Sorry, but that was a good throw." She turned her slightly rueful smile on Jeri. "No time to dally. Don't forget favors, hon."

She hit the gas and took off as Landers searched for the misplaced marble.

Jeri admired his huge form. She and Aggie

were the only straight singles in The Marauders and Jeri had quietly checked out Landers on previous runs before.

She decided to help him out and let Clyde carry the team front-runner responsibilities a while. She wheeled around to the far side of him, scanning the shrub-dotted terrain in fading sunlight.

"Figures it'd be the black marble, huh?" she said.

Landers just muttered "I'll find it" and scoured the dark ground with his darker eyes.

Jeri heard revving at her back and turned to see Brent and Aggie cresting the hill more or less in tandem.

"Here comes the bitch," she said to Landers. She turned back around and saw that – indeed – he *was* big enough to lean down and pick up the misplayed marble. "Damn," she said, staring at his broad ass, "nice…eyes."

They ended up driving off together just ahead of Brent and Aggie's arrival.

"Two fuckin' marbles left!" Jeri heard Aggie shout well behind her back. "Shit!"

She looked over at Landers.

"What the hell?" she hollered. "You guys weren't in the lead?"

He glanced over at her, met her gaze and shook his head, smiling oddly.

"Who is then?" Jeri yelled.

Landers shrugged.

"Thanks Chatty Cathy."

Jeri hit the throttle to keep pace with Landers' titanic ride.

They rode over the next hill to the west, which was open to that direction and thus considerably lighter even though the sun had already set. Right away the pair saw Sharla and Mac at the next marble jar; not only that but well beyond them someone else was off their bike and apparently hustling to yet another one. From the heavy looks of the guy and his lumbering gait Jeri guessed it had to be Zeke. She did some figuring in her head as she and Landers homed in on the jar that Sharla and Mac were now leaving behind.

"The way I figure it Gabby," she said a few moments later as she was handing him one of the pink marbles, "right now either Lou or Fred is in the lead."

"It's Gibby."

"Huh? You spoke!"

"The name's Gibby, not Gabby."

Jeri smiled. "Short for Gibson?"

"No."

That was all he said. Jeri's smile faded. "You're a weird one Land…er, Gibby."

An angrily over-revving engine filled the small valley with its hornet buzz. Landers and Jeri looked around and saw Aggie's bike streaking down the hill behind her. She remained alone as she hurtled toward them.

"People are cheating!" she was shrieking as she approached. "No one's supposed to hand out marbles."

Jeri shrugged. "No rules about that either way," she said, and she took off after Landers hoping she'd gravel-sprayed her team leader.

The dark was settling in. Chill winds were pushing through the open-sided valley from the ocean now. At the next jar Jeri risked a glance back and saw that Brent still hadn't crested the previous ridge.

"I hope your lead man's okay," she said to Landers as she handed him an orange marble.

Landers glanced back.

"Mighta given up," he rumbled under his breath. "Has before."

"You gonna check? I wouldn't trust Aggie to…"

"Prob'ly took a shortcut. He's got a phone."

Landers revved his engine. "Ready?"

"I guess if you're not worried about him then I'm not."

They took off with Aggie hot on their trail. She more or less pulled even with them before the next jar.

"You people shouldn't be handing out marbles," she said as she hustled over to the jar. "It's every man for himself out here."

"Speaking of men," Jeri said. "Where's Brent?"

"Behind me," Aggie said without taking her

eyes off her work. “That’s all that matters.”

Setting the jar and its remaining marble down, she hustled back to her bike. Jeri and Landers were already kicking off again.

The three were virtually dead even now. They could see Sharla and Mac departing the next jar’s spot, both riders and land tinged a fading orange. Dead ahead of them, bathed in the rusted light of dying day, loomed Mainerd’s Point: a true “lover’s leap” in that the promontory actually hung out over the sea. A tunnel ran through it far below, making it the only spot for many miles where no road had to be crossed to reach the Pacific’s cold black waves. Mainerd’s Point almost always featured a jar because everyone loved the view and the feel of being up on the apex of that split and knobby crag.

Jeri saw a rider ascending the steep slope leading up to the point. Had to be Zeke, she figured. She rode on and watched as he reached the summit, made a semicircle up there and then set his bike on its stand. Sharla and Mac were riding up the hill by that point and Jeri and Landers were nearly to its base. Jeri lost sight of Zeke and glanced to her right just in time to see Aggie scowling at her.

“What the hell, bitch?” Aggie spat. “You fuckin’ this guy or something? Quit playing house and get the lead out woman!”

Not waiting for a reply she opened the throttle full and her ride chewed into the hillside.

Jeri gunned it too, feeling indignant and more

than a little embarrassed. Certainly Landers had heard that.

Mac and Sharla were just getting on their bikes as Jeri and Aggie roared up neck and neck. Landers had fallen back a little.

"Still handing out marbles Sharbitch?" Aggie sniped as she dismounted.

"Not to you, dickette," Sharla shot back with a grin. And she sped off.

"Can't stand that woman," Aggie said as she and Jeri went over and picked one red marble each out of the jar.

"No point getting too worked up," Jeri said. "She's not gonna win either."

"Anybody could," Aggie said. "Lou cuts corners every time. You know that. He's probably skipped a couple to finish first."

"Where'd he learn that, do you think?" Jeri said dryly.

"Whose side are you on anyway?" Aggie said.

"The good guys, of course."

Landers pulled up. Aggie watched to see if Jeri would hand him a marble. She didn't.

Instead Jeri went back over to her bike, opened a saddle bag and pulled out a cell phone.

"What are you doing?" Aggie said. "We've got a race to finish."

"You and I don't figure into the finish. Lou may have skipped a few, but what about good old Fred? Fred is a pain in the ass."

"Fred's shit. He probably dogged Lou and ended up missing a few stops too."

"He finished third last year."

"So? You finished second the year before. And why are we wasting time on this?!"

"You go," Jeri said. "I'm gonna check on Brent."

"How? You got his number too? How many of these guys are you doing?"

"I'm calling Peg. She's got everyone's cell number, remember?"

Jeri had suspected for a while now that Aggie was a little off. In the next moment she discovered to her horror that she'd been envisioning a molehill where in fact there sat a great mountain.

"What the fuck Ags!?"

Even in the graying orange haze Jeri looked ashen. The gun in Aggie's tense grip had drained its target's blood as surely as Count Dracula.

"It was an accident."

"What? What was an accident? Where's Brent?"

"We locked up on a turn."

She was staring right through Jeri, not at her; that is, until Landers strode up.

"That's far enough Frankenstein," she said as she deflected her aim his way.

He came to a halt beside Jeri.

"You two make a cute couple," Aggie said. "Short-lived, I'm afraid, but cute."

“What are you doing?” Jeri said. “Have you lost your mind?”

Aggie grinned maniacally, her neat rows of teeth glinting.

“Kinda, yeah,” she said, apparently without a trace of regret. “Shit happens.”

“Is Brent …?”

“Dead? Yeah. Broken neck. Bad landing, I guess.”

“Oh shit,” Jeri said. “Oh holy hell. This is bad.”

“Tell me about it.”

“Look, it was an accident. You said so yourself. Put the gun down. Nobody’s going to send you to the chair for an accident.”

“Probably not,” Aggie said, letting the gun sag an inch or so, “but there’s a little more to it than that. And at this point I don’t see how what I’m about to do is going to make things any worse. There’s a major undertow here. They won’t even find you.”

Jeri had been nudging closer but Aggie raised the pistol again – her eyes wide, their pale irises painted a hellish orange by the sunset.

“Get on your hogs,” she said. “I can’t drive three of them away from here.”

Jeri glanced over at her ride, tears streaking down her cheeks. She looked back at Aggie.

“No Aggie,” she said. “Please …”

“Look, I can ride the bikes off the peak one at a time after you’re gone either way. I’m in pretty good shape. I'm just giving you a chance to go out in style."

"Nooo ...!"

"Yeeeessss I'm afraid. No witnesses."

"You're not thinking of everyone at the beach. What, you're going to kill us because you accidentally killed Brent? Have you completely lost it?"

"Oh, I'd say so. Tip of the iceberg. You'll see. Or rather you won't. Sorry. My bad."

Landers stepped in front of Jeri, blocking her from Aggie's sight.

Aggie guffawed.

"I guess you *are* a little too thick for a two-for-one shot at that," she said to him. "But no worries: I've got LOTS of bullets."

Landers strode forward.

Aggie fired two shots in rapid succession. Both hit the big hulk in the upper chest. He staggered back. Jeri caught him but he was so large that he pushed her back too.

"Oh my god Aggie!" Jeri cried, leaning out around Landers' side. "Stop it! You're insane!"

"Exactly," Aggie said, and she fired again and tore another hole into Landers' chest.

Landers fell back again, pushing Jeri along with him.

He backpedaled slowly.

"Land…er, Gibby…" Jeri said, "…watch out… we don't have much room…"

"Just keep going big guy," Aggie said, advancing. "Don't make me drag your bodies."

Landers did something completely bizarre in the next moment.

He turned and swept Jeri up into his arms. Surprised, Aggie held her fire; that is, until she saw Landers start to run. Then she hit him in the back with three more rounds. But it didn't slow him much.

He leapt off the cliff.

Aggie rushed up to the spot where he'd gone over bearing Jeri in his arms.

Hundreds of feet below the whitecaps churned between projecting rocks.

"Weird move," she said over the rushing coastal breeze. "Still effective."

Once she'd ditched the bikes in the same rugged waters she got back on hers. Brent's body and bike were all that was left between her and a clean getaway.

Well, not counting her ex. The guy who started all this. The cops might eventually find his shallow grave but it would take a while. And Stefan had no immediate-family and no job.

She headed back toward where her silencer-muzzled weapon had put an end to Brent's smugness. She'd always detested him and the opportunity had presented itself in such a timely manner that she hadn't been able to refuse.

The one thing she hadn't figured on was the darkness. Not even the glint of Brent's bike chrome presented itself to her eyes.

Growing more frantic with each passing moment she finally decided to switch her headlight on. The bright beam scoured the land ahead for a bike, or at least a prone body.

Instead it found an upright one.

Landers loomed before her. Despite her confusion and disbelief Aggie gunned it, figuring on running him down.

He stood firm.

She floored it.

She may as well have hit a brick wall. The front tire went between Landers' legs and Landers caught her by the neck as his lower body absorbed the impact.

He staggered back but a half step, barely fazed.

Holding a gasping Aggie at arms' length, relaxing his hold only as necessary to keep from suffocating her, he climbed onto her bike and rode off toward Mainerd's Point. The darkness didn't seem to bother him at all. Aggie clutched feebly at his thick arm.

He set the bike on its stand and carried her up to the summit, her arms flailing helplessly.

He relaxed his grip and let her gasp out, "Why?"

He grinned at her.

"Let's just say I've got too much of my dad in me," he said. "Oh, and Jeri's fine by the way."

He chucked Aggie off the cliff.

She splattered on a rock.

"Aw, too bad," Gil "Gibby" Landers said. "If I'd been more than half gill-man you might have cleared the rocks."

BRING DOWN THE CURTAIN

BY: KENT HILL

From the bowels of the Paris opera house

To the bright lights of Broadway

His rise to stardom

And a generous payday

From skulking, disfigured genius

In a mask that's now iconic

He longed for sneaky homicide

Now isn't that ironic

~

He killed himself, each evening

Not forgetting matinees

He'd be up all night drinking

Then sleeping half the day

"If only I could get arrested . . .

. . . perhaps lop off someone's head?

Give me a quiet prison cell

And two days sleeping like the dead."

~

So the Phantom set himself to the task

To be torn from the marquee

He sharpened well, his murderous wit

And commenced his killing spree

It wasn't long till panic struck

The daily papers would recount

They spoke of the lethal opera ghost

And the increasing body count

~

But while the people flocked to hear

Webber's music of the night

The law wouldn't lift a finger

As though crippled by stage fright

"O double damn and curse the air!"

The Phantom he was pissed

As he'd severed abducted celebrities

Thinking surely, they'd be missed

~

Sadly though, the more he killed

Indulging blood-soaked thrill

He was no match for the cash machine

His show, theatrical

So he thought he'd try a different tact

And started being rude

He'd crawl on stage all sloppy-drunk

Performing in the nude

~

The audiences seemed oblivious

They didn't boo or hiss

Even when he flopped it out

On the front row, took a piss

The critics called him bold and brash

A performer without peer

He wiped his ass with glowing praise

And cavorted with a sneer

~

At wits end and losing it

"How can I win their rage?"

He contemplated the Finnish thing

To have sex live, on stage

So on next taking to the boards

He went for the obscene

In the midst of the elegant seduction

He commenced *really* humping sweet Christine

~

The audience were not shocked at all

They'd been reading the reviews

All this did was make them return in droves

Make traffic jams of theatre cues

The Phantom trashed his dressing room

In short, he threw a fit

He came late to the following matinee

And on stage took a shit

~

Into his mic he changed the songs

'Night unfurls its splendour . . .

If that pretty boy doesn't quit Christine

I'll shove his cock into a blender'

'You alone . . .

. . . can make my song, take flight

Christine . . . you better . . .

Give me a blow job to – night

~

Pretty soon he was on the news

His life relegated to hell's pits

A pirated copy hit the net

In 2 minutes, 2 billion hits

The next night he merely sat on stage

No singing, wanked instead

After Christine slipped into her boat-shaped resting place

He cut off the bitch's head

~

The people applauded on their feet

One patron, in pants peed

He brought the head on for the curtain call

Cried as he watched it bleed

Taking to the wings, his mood most black

Stabbing the pompous prick conductor

The orchestra then took him out for drinks

Turns out, they hated the motherfucker

~

Finally he didn't emerge at all

Stopped bathing, felt real cruddy

Tried to stop the show from going on

By killing off his under-study

No more pandering to the crowds

No more product placement

But the company just threw out more cash

He could perform it from the basement

~

He'd at last reached the end of his rope

And no amount of wealth

Could raise the Phantom from his funk

He was going to kill himself

As he looked upon the hangman's noose

He knew it was time to go

His only hesitation was

How they'd work it into the show

~

No the opera ghost did not end there

Though inside he was hurtin'

He prayed earnestly for a missile strike

To bring down the final curtain

But soon there came, a new train wreck

A flame demented hubris sparked

New crap brought him mediocrity

Spider-Man: Turn off the Dark

~

Turns out the break he needed

Was not spilling blood by his own hand

He just needed his thunder stolen by

The stupidest musical in the land

He retired to the south of France

Caught up on his reading

He lounged about on sunny days

The tan he was sorely needing

~

You never saw a happier man

Free from all that sex and death

His career a distant memory

No more opera on his breath

Escaping from the limelight

Was a most exerting chore

In an insane world, if you're bat-shit weird

They'll want you all the more.

MISSING

BY: TOM LUCAS

I sat, slowly dying, in a bakery on Mack Avenue.

My fiancé conducted a rapid-fire negotiation with the owner over a counter covered with crumbs and icing, the casualties of our Monday afternoon tasting. They were debating the specific parameters of our wedding cake. There was no escape from her high-pitched whine or the chef's staccato French-Canadian accent. My only comfort was in my shallow, quick breaths.

"You ask too much," he said.

"You offer too little," she responded. "There's no way we are paying that much for the cake. There's hardly anything to it. It's a simple white on white with the damn sugar statue on top."

This went on for a while. I killed the time by

staring at the complicated pastries in the display case and fantasizing about being at work preparing the weekly reports. I fiddled with my watch. I played with my phone.

Eventually, she defeated him. That's her style. She doesn't lose. She stays in it until the battle has been won. That's why we're engaged. She always gets want she wants or she simply makes life miserable for the competition until they surrender. I wasn't much of a challenge. She made it clear to me that if we didn't get married she was out the door. I caved almost instantly.

The chef, leaning on the counter in exhaustion, turned to me. "This woman of yours, she is a wolf in sheep's clothing, my friend." He shook his head as he walked away.

Annie giggled as she sported her trademark victorious grin. I wasn't sure completely what had happened, but it seemed as if we had a reasonably priced cake to mark off the list. She grabbed my arm and we walked out to the parking lot. It was just past sunset. How long had we been in there?

"Hey, look at me," she said.

I had been staring at my shoes.

"This went well, but we have a bunch more places to hit this week. You barely said a word in there. I need you on top of this. I'm pretty much planning this wedding by myself and I won't have that," she said.

It was true. I was only along for the ride.

"Now go home, don't turn on that stupid game of yours and get some sleep. You need to go in early tomorrow because we'll be trying out wedding bands at 3:30 downtown."

"Yes, straight to bed." I found agreeing with her tended to reduce the amount of time she would talk at me.

"I'm serious. You're 29 years old, Pete. Adult time."

I nodded.

"Good. Might as well as get used to it. That game is not coming with us when we get the house," she said.

She gave me a kiss on the cheek, a half hug, and got in her car. I watched her drive away. I paused as I put the key into the ignition. Annie never seemed to second-guess herself. I was overwhelmed, adrift.

The marriage was a desperate play on my part. I haven't had much confidence dating or even talking to women. Annie had taken notice of me and handled the whole courtship, guiding me through every step. When she told me we were getting married, I said, "Sure, sounds good."

Annie wanted a man she could control, and I'm not much work. Now she had me all tied up. My future was set out before me. Marriage, then the house, then two new cars, then a trip, then two to three kids. She put it out on the table, told me the terms, and gave me her victory smile. She was the only girl who had not walked out after the first week, complaining of boredom, and it occurred to me that this was probably my only chance. I said, "ok."

After I returned home from the cake tasting, I played video games until five in the morning. I played every one I owned. It was an attempt at overdose by video game. It didn't work.

#

I had maybe an hour of sleep and starting the next day was rough, but I made it into the office early and started working the numbers. The numbers, they always treated me well. They never made me feel 'less than'. That's an old accountant joke.

Gilbert, my cubicle co-pilot, rolled in at 9:20. He's everything I'm not. Good looking, outgoing, athletic, fabulously single. His side of the cube is a complete mess and he has no regrets about it.

"What's happening, dude?" he asked as he threw his bag down on his desk. "How'd the cake thing go?"

I didn't look up. "It was so tedious. She argued for hours about every little thing. I couldn't wait to get out of there."

He chuckled. "You're not even married yet and she owns you. I warned you. Look at me, not a care in the world. I hook up on my own schedule."

I went for my coffee and found myself staring at the mug. I focused on the Arizona state logo with a cartoon coyote on it since I couldn't look him in the eyes. I wanted to set him straight, but I couldn't find anything to say. I picked up my coffee mug. I wanted to be far away, from Gilbert, Detroit, and my responsibilities.

Arizona was as good a place as any. The desert -- vast, open, and no one around for miles. There's just me and maybe my camera. It's hot, quiet, and empty. Peaceful. Then, a voice suddenly broke through my beautiful daydream. Gilbert. My desert disappeared.

"Then again, I've never heard you talking much about the ladies. Maybe better to lock one down. You keep her out in the field, and you know what happens?" he asked.

I sighed. "No, what happens?"

He raised his arms, making claws with his hands. "One day, she's out there and she meets the big, bad wolf. And then you never see her again." Gilbert seemed very pleased with this scenario.

"Thanks for that."

"It could happen. It has happened."

"Shut up, Gilbert."

"Seriously, right over in Grosse Pointe, where you're getting married. There's a great story about a werewolf that steals brides on their wedding day. They never see him coming, and they never find the bride," he said.

"I've lived in Detroit my whole life and I've never heard that story." I was starting to get pissed.

“That’s because you live in your own little world, Pete. There’s a lot of interesting stuff out there, if you would just pay attention.”

“That’s enough. I’ve got a lot to do today.” I started leafing through the stack of papers on my desk, searching for purpose.

Gilbert strapped on his headphones, so I knew I wouldn’t have to face any more of his confident guy crap for a while.

I looked at Gilbert. Not a care in the world. What a jerk. Stupid stories.

I wished that he would lose his confidence, just for a moment. Perhaps by a nasty result of his care-free lifestyle. He must have known I was picturing him in a doctor’s office complaining his urine burned because he turned towards me with an uncharacteristic frown. I tried to look like I was shuffling papers but it was not convincing.

“Crap,” he said, pulling off his headphones. “We have that stupid meeting in five minutes.”

The meeting was as boring as the cake tasting, but at least I didn’t have Annie jamming my eardrums with her demands. Mr. Archange, my supervisor, spent three hours going over our company’s imminent take over of Simonet Industries, some agricultural distributor. He droned on and on. The monotony was further supported by pie charts and graphs. The presentation, if nothing else, was consistent.

I have never been a fan of meetings. I am rarely

called upon to add to them. Today, I knew he would never ask me to quote a report or offer a number. I could hide behind my laptop and look busy while I handled several of Annie's requests: follow up emails to the caterer, checking on our invitations, and most importantly, keeping up the wedding website.

Annie thinks this stuff takes me all day. I have her fooled. I know my way around these things. I had her to-do list knocked out before Archange hit his seventh slide. Now I could relax and resume my hunt for a better video card. My gaming addiction is severe and I am always playing catch up. As a precaution, I spared a moment to check-in on the progress of the meeting.

Archange made several important points. He always curls up his right hand into a fist and punches the air. That's the cue to nod like you're paying attention. A little bit of eye contact, and then back to whatever you were doing.

I had made my way through eBay listings, a few tech forums, and had finally reached the riskiest of sources, Craigslist Detroit. Usually nothing but scam artists and prostitutes. And no, I don't go for anything like that. I would catch AIDS from the first time out. That's the kind of luck I have. Or I would be robbed, killed, or arrested.

There weren't any decent listings in the computer section and the boss was just now rounding second in his presentation. I was about to end my search and start tweeting about the coffee stain on Gilbert's tie when I happened to notice "Weddings" on the page. Funny, I had never noticed that before.

Most of the listings were for wedding dresses, used once or never. But there was one strange one, "Wedding Extractions".

Ok, weird. I had to click on it.

There wasn't much to it. Just a name, Louis G., and a number. I jotted it down. It was curious.

#

Another afternoon and evening completely gone.

Annie and I spent four hours listening to wedding bands audition. These poor bands – no one was going to live up to Annie's standards. We listened to a rock band, a piano player/singer combo, and three R & B groups. Each group had to present three songs: one ballad, one party starter, and OUR SONG.

The auditions were trials of pain and agony. The rock band nailed the ballad with Bon Jovi's "Wanted Dead or Alive" but crashed and burned on OUR SONG. The piano player/singer failed on all counts but OUR SONG. The R&B groups? When it came to the party starters, they nailed it. One group turned out "Unchained Melody" to the point where Annie started to mist up. But no one could truly play OUR SONG.

It was really Annie's song. She picked it, and told me what it was going to be. I had no input in the matter. I would not have picked "Run For Your Life" by the Beatles. She apparently didn't pick up on:

"Well I'd rather see you dead, little girl
Than to be with another man
You better keep your head, little girl
Or I won't know where I am"

I will never understand how she didn't figure out this song. She liked the melody, I suppose.

Surprisingly, she was rather polite, almost sweet, with the bands as she dismissed them. She offered them some hope that they might be hired for the gig. Knowing her facial expressions as I do, I knew that no one had made the cut and we would be spending the weekend looking for more.

After the band auditions, we shuffled off to Grosse Pointe Academy, our wedding venue. Although I had no say in this choice either, Annie did well here. The Academy had been built in 1889 and was filled with stained glass, rich woodwork, and it was on Lake St. Clair. We were to have the wedding in the chapel and the reception on the lake. It reminded me quite a bit of the final scene of Dustin Hoffman's *The Graduate*. Everything was going to be just as Annie had always imagined it.

She wanted to do some measurements and look at the pew width of the chapel so she could accurately plan out the seating arrangements. "Pete, just go sit in the back row and keep your eye on me. I want to understand the sight lines," she said.

I was happy to help. Sitting in the farthest pew meant I could fiddle with my phone and kill some time.

"So how does it look back there?" she asked. The echo was incredible. Her voice bounced off of every surface and drilled deep into my ears.

"Good dear," I mumbled. I wasn't even looking. She didn't care. She was already measuring the distance between the altar and the dais. I needed a rescue from this personal hell.

In my mind's eye, I pictured a large hand plucking off the dome of the chapel and scooping her up. She screamed and flung her arms, but to no avail. I pretended to jump to try to pull her down, but in my dream's reality, I was only standing on my tiptoes. Her voice trailed off as the hand retracted, pulling her into the abyss.

I felt a presence standing over me. It was Annie. Time to look invested.

"Earth to Pete. Hello?" she said.

I sat up straight. "Ha ha, sweets. Do you have the measurements you wanted?"

"Pete, it's critical that you stay plugged into this. I need your input. Now we're done in here. Time to go outside."

It would be harder to hide now, but you have to do what you have to do. We headed out the majestic double doors out to the grounds where the reception would take place.

We were standing in the middle of the well-manicured lawn between the chapel and the lake. I could see Annie mentally plotting the position of each table, tent, and the dance floor. She had a great mind for this, much better than mine. I know this because she told me.

Annie was winding up and I could tell that I was about to receive a barrage of items for tomorrows to-do list. Before she could take a breath, a silver-haired grandmother-type interrupted us. Dressed in professional attire, it was clear that she worked for the academy.

"Annie and Pete?" she asked.

Annie turned away from me in mid-thought. "There you are! I thought we had been forgotten."

The older woman either didn't realize that Annie was passively complaining or didn't care. She had a grace about her. Grosse Point Academy was most assuredly filled with entitled brats from the old money of Detroit's East Side. Annie would hardly register as demanding.

"Hello dear, I'm Bonnie. I'm here to help you with any questions you have about the facility," she said.

"Good, good," replied Annie. "We're actually set with the inside. I have a few questions about the reception area."

Bonnie listened intensely as Annie went through a long list of minute details. She seemed to have everything covered, from electrical outlets to bathrooms. Her level of planning would have been impressive if I hadn't been bored into a stupor. It was just another conversation where I would have nothing to say.

Then she asked Bonnie if they could move a rather large boulder that sat on the water's edge. It was Bonnie's dismissive laughter that brought me back from daydream land.

"Oh dear, that boulder isn't going anywhere. It's been here for over 250 years, " she said.

Annie frowned. "It destroys the sight line."

Bonnie looked over at the over-sized rock. It couldn't have been more than three feet high, maybe 8 feet wide. She looked back at Annie, clearly annoyed. Ok, there was a chip in her graceful armor.

"It's hardly a worry. Once you have your tents and floral arrangement out here, it will blend in nicely," she said dryly.

"Pete, go run out there and stand next to that thing," Annie said. She wasn't quite ready to let this one go.

Bonnie let out a very quiet sigh. I trotted out to the rock and dutifully stood beside it.

"It's nearly half as tall as he is," Annie said, clearly frustrated.

She started negotiating some kind of rock removal fee, but I tuned it out. The boulder, really just a big rock, was well worn and the bottom half of it was covered in a fine moss. It had a strong smell, an old smell. It was comforting. There were deep grooves cut into the rock from a few centuries of rain. This rock had sat here for sometime looking out onto the lake. I ran my hand along its surface. It was then I noticed a strange impression. It was somewhat oval, and there were four smaller circles above it. It looked like a paw print.

I carefully examined it. It was definitely a paw print. That wasn't even remotely possible. This was solid stone. The impression looked like it had been pressed in, like a big dog's paw in wet concrete. There was something familiar about it. It tugged at my mind. Wasn't there something Gilbert had said...?

I didn't have a lot of time to think about it. Annie was done with Bonnie and headed back to the car. It took a bit of effort but I managed to catch up with her. The car ride home was very quiet. I had expected Annie to use the time to revisit my to-do list and complain about the ineptitude of Bonnie and the Academy staff. Her silence was unnerving.

Annie pulled up to my apartment building. She put the car into park and turned to me. The soft light from the streetlight bounced off her eyes.

"I know I have been tough to be around, but this wedding needs to be exact. You know me, I get tough about the important things," her voice so soft it was almost a whisper. This was as close as Annie ever came to an apology.

"It's okay," I said.

She smiled.

I hadn't seen that in a while. It wasn't her victory smile. It was the simple smile that she gave me when I first told her that I loved her.

I gave her a quick kiss.

"Good. Just a few weeks left," she said happily.

The reality of the upcoming ceremony, which I had no input on even though she said she wanted some, was like being splashed with cold water. It washed away the warm moment, and left me feeling numb. "Just a few weeks left," sounded more like a doctor telling me how long I had to live. I walked inside, exhausted. It wasn't late enough to go to sleep, so I killed some time online gaming, looking for computer parts, and screwing around on Facebook. I was trying to ignore the piece of paper that had Louis's phone number scrawled on it. It sat on the desk next to me, almost screaming.

Wedding Extractions.

What did that mean, 'wedding extractions'? Did Louis pilot a helicopter, pulling grooms to safety? Like the fall of Saigon? Did men stand on church domes scrambling to get on the swaying rope ladder as he waved from the cockpit?

Or was he more like a dentist pulling out a rotten tooth?

I picked up my phone and started to dial. I set the phone back down. I did this three more times -- between a game, a snack, and a quick walk around my building. It was the fifth time that I dialed that I let it ring.

He picked up immediately. “Hallo?”

“Lou-is?” I asked.

“Ha ha,” he said. “It’s Lou-ee.” He had a strong French-Canadian accent, just like the pastry chef. Odd. “How can I help you?”

“It’s not too late is it?” I stammered.

“No, my friend. I live for the night.”

“I’m calling about your ad on Craigslist? Wedding extractions?”

“Of course. I am more than happy to help,” he said.

“I, uh, well…” I couldn’t even finish.

“I can give you all the answers you need, my friend. Let’s meet. Tomorrow?”

“Tomorrow is fine.”

“Excellent. Do you know Hamtramck? Meet me at Café 1923 at dusk,” he said. “Until tomorrow. Good bye.”

Dusk?

#

I was having a hard time focusing my thoughts. I couldn’t get my mind off Louis. Why did I call him? Should I even meet him? Thankfully, Gilbert came in early and quickly got me out of my head. I had my nose in some spreadsheets, not really seeing the numbers, when Gilbert leaned over the wall of our cubicle.

"Hey buddy," he said. Donut crumbs fell from his mouth.

"Morning, Gilbert." I didn't look up.

"So hey man, not too much longer. You're going to be locked up without a key," he said.

I winced. "Yep, that's going to be me."

"You know, you did name me best man, and I know you don't want to have a bachelor party."

I looked up sharply. "You have better not made any plans. Annie will castrate me."

"Relax. I asked around." Gilbert leaned in. "Uh, none of the guys here really wanted to go out anyway," he said apologetically.

"Gee, thanks for that."

"Aw, I didn't mean it like that. ok, it's exactly how it sounds. What I'm trying to say is that I want to take you out for a few beers. We've done that before, but you need at least one more outing before the gates close before you," he said.

"Fine. Just no strip clubs. No way," I said.

Gilbert straightened up and shook his head. "No sir. I was thinking of this German place on the East Side. 30 year-old scotch. Maybe a cigar."

"So a refined evening? That's acceptable."

Gilbert smiled. "Atta boy! I'll figure out a night for it. Now let's get to crunching some numbers."

It wasn't a bad idea, and satisfying Gilbert's need to 'save me' if only for an evening was admirable. He was the closest thing I had to a friend.

The remainder of the day was blissfully busy. I didn't have much time to think about my meeting with Louis. By the time I had wrapped up work, the sun was starting to sink.

Dusk.

#

Café 1923 is right across the street from the old Kowalski meat plant in Hamtramck. Hamtramck used to be a predominantly Polish neighborhood, and the big neon sausage skewered by a fork that hangs over its doors is a local landmark. The sign hasn't worked in years. I found a parking spot underneath it, mainly so I could see my car from the café.

The sun had already gone down so I rushed into the coffeehouse. It was a hipster haven, and it was packed. I grabbed a quick cup of coffee as I scanned the room. It was filled with people clicking away on laptops or reading books and there was too much conversation. I realized that Louis had never described himself. I felt flustered, almost panic mode.

The café was filled with young, pretty people. They all looked far more interesting than me. They all sported colorful, ironic t-shirts. Funky hats. Inventive forms of facial hair. I was surprised they didn't kick me out for being so boring. Once my eyes focused, I found Louis. It had to be Louis. With a flannel shirt, muscular build, and thick beard, he looked just as out of place as I did. I took the empty seat across from him at the table.

"Hello? Louis?" I asked.

"Why yes, you must be my appointment," he said. His voice was rough and deep. A voice ideal for radio, but his accent would probably make it challenging for him. "You are looking for a wedding extraction, correct?"

"Yes."

A subtle smile formed under his beard. His whiskers bristled. "You do not love this woman?" he asked.

"Yes, umm, no. I do love her but she is too much for me," I said.

"Too much of a woman?" He chuckled. "You cannot handle her?"

"No."

"Perhaps you need some love-making lessons? It's important to keep the appetite satisfied," he offered.

He was taunting me. "I'm sure I don't need the lessons. It's not about that."

"Ah, so what is the problem? Specifics, please."

"I am in over my head. She's very controlling and we are not even married yet. I know that I am doomed to a life of sheepish servitude," I sighed.

"So you wish the wedding canceled?"

"Yes."

"I see. You want a wedding extraction?"

"I think so, but I'm not really sure what that

means," I said.

"Ah, well. It is a solution to your problem, my friend. I pull the wedding away from you." He made a violent pulling gesture.

I had no idea what that meant. "Go on."

"Yes. That is it. I pull the wedding away from you. No wedding. Ever. At least not for you and your woman."

"It's that simple?"

"It is."

"Is it expensive? I don't have a lot of money," I said. My voice cracked.

"I do not accept money. However, there is always a price. This is true of all things," he said.

"So there is a price?"

"Yes. Always a price."

"What is the price?" I asked.

"Do you love this woman? Surely you do. You must."

"Yes, I said that." I was getting a bit frustrated. He was definitely toying with me.

"The price – the price is that she will never marry you after I have performed the extraction. She will never love you again. Not for a day. There will be no second chance for love."

I chewed on my lip. Never? Louis leaned back in his chair and stretched his arms out.

"Never? Gone forever?"

Louis leaned in and spoke softly. "The price is that you must live with the consequences of your request."

"Wow. Can I think about this?" I asked.

"No. I can tell you are…" He stroked his beard. "…wishy-washy. Now is the time to decide. Time to do something." He made a fist and knocked loudly on the table.

He wasn't going to give me too much time to think. I rubbed my eyes, attempting to release all of the stress of the wedding, Annie, and my worries for the future. I'm not sure how much time had passed before I spoke again, but the world I pictured without her was more peaceful and relaxing. It was lonely, but quiet.

"Ok," I said.

"Yes? You mean yes? You want the extraction?"

"I do."

"Fine. It is done. You will have it," he said with a slight smile. "All you must do is invite me to the wedding. I will handle the rest."

I cringed. How would I explain him to Annie? He didn't even remotely look like someone I would have as a friend.

"It may be tough. I know," he said. "But you must. This is all you have to worry about. I will take good care of you. Do not worry about anything." He stood up, his large frame casting a shadow over me. "I will protect you," he said.

#

Soon it was the day before the wedding. The previous few weeks had gone by without incident, but were jammed with a ridiculous amount of trivial details that Annie insisted on adjusting and readjusting. I began to think that she is just the kind of person that is never satisfied, and that realization was very depressing.

It wouldn't be long after we are married when she will look at me over the dinner table and understand that I didn't have any extra levels, and that I would most likely never be anything more than I am now – an underweight, passive-aggressive egghead with a penchant for avoiding conflict and fast food. At that point she'd have an affair and then find a lawyer. I'll end up where I'm at now, but with less money and an arrow labeled "cuckold" floating over my head. Today was the last day Annie would not see the real me, only what she wanted to see.

It was also my last day of work for two weeks. The boss had been merciful and gave me a light workload. Gilbert had been in meetings all day. If I could manage to avoid him, I would be free and clear of any plans he had made for us. I tried to work away from the cubicle after lunch, and made good use of the employee lounge.

It didn't matter. He caught me in the parking lot as I was about to head home.

He shouted from two lanes over. "Dude! Tonight's the night. Your last night of freedom. Are you ready?"

I started to fiddle with my keys. "Yeah, right. You know, I've got a bunch of things to take care of."

Gilbert closed the distance. He was now standing in front of me, sporting his serious face. "You're lying. I've seen you mark off the items on your to-do list. You don't have anything left to do but go out with me," he said.

"ok, you got me. Where are we going?"

"German joint on the East Side. Haus des Wolfs. They've got that 30 year-old scotch I was telling you about. Gonna treat you right." Gilbert smiled and got into his car.

I rushed home to get ready. I'm not much for going out. I went through the closet. I grabbed my trusty yellow Polo and jeans. Seemed good enough.

My phone rang. I looked down at the screen.

Annie.

"Hey sweetie, I was just about to call you. Gilbert –"

She had no time for hellos. "Pete, do you have your tux hanging out? I can't have wrinkles."

Another detail. I took a deep breath to calm my annoyance and looked over at my tux. It was hanging over a chair. "Yes, it's hanging up."

"ok, I just know that you never pay attention to your clothes," she said. "What's this about Gilbert? What did he screw up?"

"Nothing, sweetie. He's taking me out for a drink," I said.

"What? You didn't mention this before." She was clearly perturbed.

"Just a boy's night out. Just me and him."

"Are you going to one of those clubs?"

"No. I would never," I said.

"Well, I think you should. This is your last chance, and let's be honest, you haven't had many chances to begin with." She laughed.

She did not have to rub it in. "I don't like those places. Just some German place. Beer and sausages, I think."

"You know Pete, this is good. You should go out. You never go out." Annie sounded happy. "Tomorrow's going to be amazing, go celebrate. Love you."

That surprised me. "Love you too. Thanks for understanding," I said.

"I'm not a monster, Pete. Have your fun."

Hanging up the phone, I took a look around the apartment. I ran my hand along the couch cushions. Still on Planet Earth. Unbelievable. I expected flames to shoot through my phone. Maybe I have just been so stuck in my head over the wedding to realize that Annie was actually a decent girl, and more pragmatic than I could ever be. She was a realist and somewhat accepting of human nature. I have always had my head up in the clouds, unable to communicate my feelings to others. Annie knew this and she still loved me.

That put a bit of a smile on my face as I finished

getting ready.

This bar that Gilbert had picked out, it was in the worst neighborhood I had ever seen. It actually wasn't all that far from where we were getting married but was down a road that looked sketchy. He sure knew how to pick them. The street the bar was on was filled with cars at least. I was forced to park on the next block.

When I got out of my car, I was struck by how quiet it was. Not a streetlight working, either – although there was one struggling to fire. Its low hum and crackle hovered overhead as I briskly walked towards the tavern.

At one time, this street was most certainly alive and bustling. Old storefronts lined up side by side, and it wasn't hard to picture people crowding the streets, socializing, having a good time. Now, nothing but broken windows. Evidence of fire damage. Doors with plywood hammered into place, covered with code violation notices from the city.

I stopped in front of a former butcher shop. The window was filthy, but cracks of light were coming through the ceiling. Pressing up against the glass, I could see a room frozen in time. The counter, the coolers, even the slicers were still in place. They were covered in dust. It was as if the owner had finished for the day, closed shop, and simply never returned.

Then I saw it. Something moved.

A flicker of shadow, then nothing.

I looked again. Nothing. I stepped back for a moment and took another look. Nothing. My neck tightened. Something was behind me.

I slowly looked to my right. Just an empty street.

I looked to my left.

The door to the bar exploded and three college-age kids stumbled out, laughing. I don't know why I have such an active imagination. I felt relieved to be back to reality. I took a deep breath and sucked in my stomach. I walked into the bar.

It was dark but charming. Very gothic, at least in an old Universal horror sort of way. It wasn't a big place, but it was filled with long, wooden common tables and a few high-backed, ornate booths in the corner. A solid oak bar ran the length of the far wall, and a stone fireplace in the back made the room feel like a traveler's inn, somewhere in the Bavarian Alps.

The patrons ranged from a few artsy types, the after-work business crowd, to a small group of dusty men gathered at one end of the bar. They looked as if they had been sitting in here since the turn of the century – the last century.

Gilbert sat at the table nearest the fireplace, and he already had a pitcher of beer and two thick glass mugs waiting. He motioned excitedly towards me. "There you are man! I was getting worried something happened to you."

I sat down next to him. I felt anxious. "Romantic seat by the fire?"

Gilbert laughed. "It's a real deal closer, I can tell you. So how ya feeling?"

"Good I think. Nervous, " I said.

He nodded. "I'd be afraid for you if you weren't."

He went on to remind me of the virtues of being single. He detailed a few of his most recent adventures. He ordered us that 30 year-old scotch he had bragged about. It wasn't too long before I had loosened up and we managed to talk about something other than the fact that I was getting married and he wasn't.

We shared a few stories about work, and our ridiculous jobs. He tried to talk sports with me, but that was a dead end. I tried to talk video games with him, but he just glazed over. The evening went by, and it was much more enjoyable than I had expected. I had been so engrossed in my conversation with Gilbert that I hardly noticed that the bar had emptied. All that remained was the bartender and two of the dusty men in the corner.

It had gotten quiet.

Gilbert was staring in the fire. "You know man, I do envy you a bit."

This was unexpected. I was a bit foggy, but he caught my attention. "How so?"

"I know I've been giving you a lot of static about getting hitched. The ball and chain stuff," he said. Gilbert turned away from the fire and pointed at my chest. "But the thing is, you found her. You found the one, maybe. Time will tell there. Still, you found her. Most people don't. I say a lot of nonsense, but don't be fooled. You got something. Keep it."

I looked into my empty mug.

He looked back into the fire. "She's a bit of a battle axe, but she's yours. Be glad for tomorrow. I'm glad for you. Cherish that. The good ones, hell, even the ok ones…they don't come around that often." Gilbert sighed. "Ah, I'm drunk. We need to get going."

"Maybe we should call for a ride?" I asked.

"No, we'll be fine. Let's just get out of here," he said.

Gilbert slowly pushed himself up from his chair, resting both hands on the table for stability. "Scotch. Ha ha."

"Are you going to be ok?" I asked.

He gave me a sloppy thumbs-up. I had my doubts.

As we shuffled towards the door, the bartender stopped washing glasses and gave us a hard look. "Your buddy ok?"

I waved yes. I was afraid to speak. I might slur my words and then we'd be stuck here waiting for a cab. There was no time for that.

One of the dusty old men looked over at us. His face was a tight web of ancient wrinkles and dirt. His long shaggy beard and his crazy eyes only served to make me feel more anxious.

"Yep, they'll make it home tonight. And this one…" He pointed at me. "Tomorrow's groom. He'll be back."

The other man and the bartender laughed. It was a bitter sound that gave me chills.

They turned away from us and we double-timed our way outside. The night had fully wrapped the street in shadows. The broken streetlights hung over us, promising nothing. I squinted and thought that maybe I could see my car. That part of the street disappeared into inky blackness.

Although I have never been too nervous about visiting the city, this street rattled me. The empty storefronts, with their boarded up or missing windows, reflected little light. They sat in silence, with nothing but blank expressions and open mouths. Looming tombs of days long past.

I must have been standing there for a while, trying to find my car before I braved the darkness. Gilbert started hitting me on the shoulder.

"Hey man, we gotta get going," He said. He sounded concerned.

I turned to Gilbert and that's when I saw them. Two men, mere silhouettes in the shadows. They were moving towards us quickly. Running.

"Hey!" one of them shouted. Gilbert ran across the street. They came up on Gilbert and began beating him. He fell to the ground. Their arms flailed down upon him. I heard a sickening crack. Black streams of blood slowly trailed from their fists into the moonless sky. Gilbert screamed and started to cover up, but they would not stop.

"Take my money, just don't hurt me anymore," Gilbert moaned.

They rummaged through his pockets, taking what little he had. Then the shadows stopped and looked at me.

"Your turn," one of them said.

I turned to run to the car. I tried to yell out to Gilbert that I was going to call for help, but the words were trapped in my throat. I couldn't see a thing. I was running clumsily down the sidewalk. I tripped and stumbled and could barely keep my balance as I built up speed. But my shoes betrayed me by finding an uneven patch of concrete. I felt a sharp pain in my ankle before it gave out and dumped me to the ground.

The men stood over me.

"Don't make us kill you. Give us what we want."

I sat up and fumbled for my wallet. My hands shook and I couldn't seem to find my pocket. Every moment I hesitated brought me closer to their fists.

Behind them, something moved. A third man? No. Gilbert? No. Something big.

"Quit stalling," one of the men said. "Don't think we're going to fall for that old trick.

The other man turned anyway. He started to speak, but all I heard was a deep growling, animal noise. Then a breath. Then he simply wasn't there.

The window of a storefront shattered. Whatever had taken him had moved quickly and had thrown him through it. There were screams, the sound of something tearing, something wet, and then nothing.

Silence. The man stood over me. What little light there was pooled into his wide-open eyes. He paused, looked at me, and ran. There was a moan coming from the abandoned store. It slowly grew in volume and force, until it erupted into a thunderous howl.

Gilbert began to crawl over to me. "Pete? Pete, you ok?"

I patted myself as if I was searching for something. "I'm ok."

"Pete, we need to go," he said.

I paused. The howl had stopped. The storefront was silent. "Yes we do."

Limping, I walked Gilbert to his car. Poor Gilbert's face was broken and he was struggling to breathe. He was covered in his own blood.

"Hospital?" I asked.

"No. Home." Gilbert put his hand on my arm. "I don't think we should tell anyone about this. That guy is dead for sure. They will never believe us."

I nodded.

"Good, um, tomorrow." he said. His voice was strained.

I got in my car and drove away. My hands

shook and could barely hold onto the wheel. The streets were strangely vacant. I never bothered to turn the radio on. The low hum of the tires thumping on the pavement carried me home.

#

I stayed in bed until noon. As Annie had taken care of so many of the details, there wasn't much for me to do or follow up on. I stared at the ceiling for hours. I had been up since six. I had no capability to process what had happened.

The phone rang. I answered. It was Gilbert.

"Hey Pete." He sounded apprehensive.

"Hi."

"Yeah. So, the day is finally here. You ready? I'm coming over in a hour," he said.

I let out a long, slow breath. "I will. I feel like I'm made of stone. Still in bed."

"Last night. You know we can't ever talk about it."

I sat up. "Never."

"Look, my face is a mess. I'm hung over. I look and feel like a bus hit me. And that's what I am going to tell people when they see me."

"You're a good friend," I said.

"Your best. Now get ready. This will all be over in a few hours. Then you'll just have the rest of your life to live with it." Gilbert laughed. "Argh. I can't laugh. Hurts too much."

I got out of bed and got busy. I went through the motions, step by step. Eventually I found myself at the chapel.

Annie's vision had turned out to be quite magical. The chapel had classic but tasteful arrangements of flowers, candles, and ribbon throughout. It was a gorgeous room to begin with, but now it was quite spectacular.

I didn't have that much time and it wasn't too long before the moment arrived. I stood at the front of the church with the priest and Gilbert. He radiated joy although his face was a sea of bruises and lacerations. His lip was split, but he still managed a grin. He was truly happy for me.

I scanned the crowd. We had invited at least 200 people. There were a lot of faces, all smiling, whispering – anticipating. Everyone dressed in their finest. I knew or had met them all. But one suddenly came into focus.

Louis.

I had forgotten all about him. Between all the last minute details of the past few weeks, last night and the whirlwind of today… I had forgotten all about him.

Louis smiled.

He looked ridiculous. He was wearing some kind of annoyingly vintage suit and top hat. He carried a cane with him.

I tried to manage a smile back. Nothing.

Louis looked to the rear of the chapel, then back

to me. He made a pulling motion with the handle of the cane. I shook my head. He nodded. I didn't want this anymore. I wanted the wedding.

The music started and Annie appeared with her father. As he walked her down the aisle, I began to feel overwhelmed. She looked amazing. It was truly her moment. Our moment. She looked so pleased as she gently stepped forward. Her dress was brilliantly white and although classic, she had not gone with the veil.

Gilbert patted me on the shoulder and whispered good luck. I looked at Louis. He had removed his top hat. His strong features, long hair, and beard contrasted his old suit in an almost comical way. His eyes were fixated on Annie. She was about to walk past him.

He glanced at me and nodded. He was an arm's reach from Annie. She turned and looked at him and a puzzled expression formed on her face. She turned her head forward, clearly angry. For one sliver of a second, it may have even been rage. It soon faded. She was back in the moment. Her moment.

Louis reached out towards her. I wanted to scream.

He lowered his arm. Louis had done nothing but watch her. He stood forward now. He nodded. He placed a finger against his brow and saluted me. He had changed his mind. He saw that I didn't want it. He gave me a second chance, even though he said he wouldn't. For once, someone listened to me.

A few more steps and then Annie stood before me. I smiled. I began to cry. She wiped a few of my tears away. The priest said his words. We said ours. We were married. I made it. It was finally over. It felt wonderful.

We moved outside. The Academy had done a great job of dressing up the lawn with tents and tables. Lake St. Clair was peaceful, almost glass. The sun bounced away from us, slowly setting. A slight breeze carried the sweet fragrance of flowers past us.

All of my nervousness was gone. Annie and I sat at our special table, looking out at all of our friends and family. Dinner had been perfect, and aside from the usual glass clinking, we had been spared any major embarrassments. Of course, there was Gilbert. He had a best man speech to deliver. He stood up from the table nearest to us, gave me a wink, and walked up to the microphone.

"Hey, is this thing on?" He tapped loudly on it.

Annie rolled her eyes, but smiled. I gave her a quick pat on the knee. Gilbert was a disaster from the neck up.

"ok, now before I get going I suppose I should say something about my somewhat rough appearance." He said.

There was some nervous laughter.

"So Pete and I went out last night…" Gilbert paused. I tightened up. Annie looked over to me.

"And I told Pete that Annie was too good for

him and I was going to stop the wedding." Gilbert smirked and pointed to his black eye. "This is what Pete had to say to that."

Gilbert got a few honest laughs in response. They were probably from those who knew I wasn't capable of fighting and hardly able to do any kind of damage like that.

Gilbert chuckled. "I'm kidding! But not about Annie." He looked over to me. "Pete, face it, she's way better than you deserve."

I nodded. It was going to be okay, Gilbert was going to keep it classy.

Annie leaned in and whispered in my ear. "I love you." I held her hand in mine and squeezed.

He went on to talk about how Annie and I met. How I changed at work. How Annie had made me a better person. He mentioned my one previous girlfriend.

A figure appeared, standing at the back of the tent.

Louis.

With all eyes up front, I was the only one who could see him. He stood there, top hat and cane, mouth quivering. He began to walk through the crowd, straight towards our table.

With his first steps, he dropped the cane and top hat. His skin began to appear darker. His brow thickened and furrowed.

People were beginning to notice him. He took a few more steps.

His jaw began to grow and push forward. There was a scream. Gilbert stopped talking and dropped the microphone. Louis' body began to change, contorting as he grew in size.

He kept moving towards us. Someone shouted for help.

He was transforming. Hair grew out from his skin, quickly covering it in a dark fur. His eyes turned blood red.

He howled.

This terrible, piercing howl came out of him as if he was in complete agony.

People began to push away from their tables in fear. They fell over each other as they ran for safety. Annie and I sat frozen. I couldn't breathe. Annie screamed. With one final push of his twisted body, his suit exploded from the seams. What remained was no longer human, but a monster.

Snarling, he flashed rows of glistening, sharp teeth and leapt towards the table. I tried to pull Annie away, but I wasn't strong enough. The sheer force of the beast knocked the table over and threw us to the ground. I refused to let go of her. I held her with all my might. I could feel his jaws clamp down onto Annie's arm.

He began to pull. Annie shouted in pain. If I held on any longer, he would surely tear her arm off.

I let go.

And with that, she was pulled away.

She was dragged off with inhuman speed. Annie couldn't stop screaming. I heard her voice for several minutes after they disappeared into the surrounding woods.

There was so much blood. So much blood.

Someone shook me. My father and his friends stood over me, furiously shouting.

Gilbert yelled. "Goddammit Pete, we have to go help her!"

"Look at all this blood!" I sat shaking. Tears filled my eyes. I hyperventilated.

I felt myself pulled up to my feet.

"We can do this, buddy. Come on," Gilbert said.

I went with the group, but my mind had shattered. I followed the search party in a stupor. We searched for hours…days…weeks. We never did find Annie, just a torn piece of her wedding dress in a pool of blood.

For months after Annie was taken, the media hounded me. I was tried and sentenced by the public, though not by a court. Her friends and family, once my biggest supporters, blamed me for her kidnapping. The longer she remained missing, the less sympathy I received.

It is the consequence of my request, and I have to live with it.

My life is now lonely and quiet. I have spent many evenings sitting by that mossy rock on the shore of Lake St. Clair. Sometimes I run my hand over the paw print embedded in its surface. I try to understand it.

Once the sun sinks below the horizon, I drive over to that German tavern and sit with the dusty old men. They never ask questions and they rarely speak. I haven't seen Gilbert in a long time and most people just avoid me. I suppose they don't know what to say.

With no one to bother me, this gives me plenty of time to think.

I miss Annie.

WILL THE REAL MONSTER PLEASE STAND UP?

BY: ROMA GRAY

Alistair Black pulled out his antique gold pocket watch and popped open the lid. A scowl crossed his face. His contact was late. Very late. Not a good sign. Should he continue to wait? What if Sahid had been intercepted by Logan? Logan's men could be on their way to kill him right now. Then again, without the Egyptian statue Sahid had stolen from the Beijing Museum, Alistair wouldn't have the next clue. And without the next clue, how would he ever find the tomb of the mysterious, unnamed Egyptian king who was referred to as the Dark Pharaoh? He had no choice; he had to wait.

Alistair's eyes carefully scanned the empty New Jersey construction site. A brilliant orange harvest moon stained everything with an eerie golden light. In the dark, unfinished houses and unrecognizable construction equipment seemed to twist together into dark, menacing shapes. It was the perfect Halloween landscape, orange against black and gray shadows.

Hidden within those shadows, Hans Garrison watched Alistair. A smile creased his face, his hands gripping and re-gripping his rifle in anticipation. As soon as the courier arrived, he and his partner would kill both men and retrieve the Egyptian statue as ordered. He signaled his partner on the other side of the site. The other man indicated that he too was ready. Logan would be pleased.

Hans enjoyed watching Alistair from the shadows, enjoyed seeing how the archaeologist had changed. It had been eight...no, nine...years since he had last seen him. Alistair was no longer the robust, brawny man he remembered. Now he looked like an over-the-hill cowboy in his ridiculous hat, faded jeans, and plaid shirt. The most interesting change, however, the one he couldn't see, was the artificial leg. Information had it that Alistair had lost his left leg in a car accident recently. After all of his adventures, how ironic was that?

The gunman thought back to the last time he had seen Alistair. On that particular day, Alistair had won the prize. Hans would never forget how his then employer had punished him for his failure. He had shot Hans in the left leg—the same leg the archaeologist had lost. He angrily recalled the pain-filled weeks he spent in the hospital. It seemed fated that their paths would cross again now. Logan had paid him a considerable sum to kill Alistair, but left the details to Hans. He smiled as his imagination formulated many different and horrific options. He would take a long time to kill Alistair— a very, *very* long time.

Suddenly, Hans realized his left leg, the one he'd been thinking about just moments before, felt warm and wet. He looked down and, to his complete astonishment, there was a large orange tabby cat, diligently spraying his leg.

He jerked back, furious. "Why you son of a—"

But before he could finish the sentence, his voice was cut off with a growl and a hiss as a lithe Russian Blue cat launched herself into his face. As the Russian Blue ripped at his face, the orange tabby tore a hole through his jeans with one swift movement of its large paw. The man screamed and accidentally hit the trigger of his automatic weapon.

To his left, Alistair heard an eruption of gunfire and saw a blast of harsh yellow light tear through the darkness. He dropped behind a trash can and cursed as his artificial leg toppled him sideways, causing his favorite hat to fall off of his head and roll into the dirt. He tried to recover from the fall, but discovered that the leg was weighing him down like an anchor, and it took all of his strength to straighten himself. Feeling his face burn with frustration, he pulled his gun out of his jacket pocket and peered around the trash can. How could he ever hope to do his job without his leg? He felt weak and frightened, a crippled old man whose days were about to come to a bloody end. Forcing the words of doubt from his mind, Alistair instead focused on the situation. Somewhere in the dark, he heard another man screaming, apparently locked in some kind of struggle, and it was then that it occurred to him that the gunfire had not been directed at him. He had expected Logan's men to pay him a visit, but who the hell was the guy fighting? Was there yet a third interested party?

A blaze of gunfire then exploded from the shadows on his right, bullets ricocheting loudly off the trash can. This time there was no mistaking it, this time he was definitely the target. He pulled his body in tighter, trying to evade the bullets. The gunfire abruptly stopped.

"Hey! Hey!" Alistair heard a pair of panicked voices, one to the left and one to the right. The voices seemed to be moving...up.

Alistair peeked around the trash can and almost dropped his gun in amazement. Two squirming men rose from the shadows and floated over the lit dirt path in front of him. At a height of approximately ten feet, all movement stopped. They were just hovering there. Then, after a few seconds had passed, the two men suddenly slammed into each other in mid-air. They cried out and cursed. Slowly, the two men were pulled apart, but they continued to hover above the ground.

"Help!" yelled one of the men to Alistair, his face bleeding with what looked like long, deep scratch marks. The man looked vaguely familiar, but Alistair couldn't quite place him. "Get us down from here!"

"Get you down?" Alistair struggled to his feet, using his black cane for leverage. "I'm still wondering how you got up there."

"They are up there because I wish it," replied a voice, hidden somewhere in the blackness of the night. "Drop your guns."

The two men searched the ground for the owner of the voice, but they did not release their weapons. Abruptly, they were jerked several feet apart and thrown together again with an audible clunk. With a yelp, they finally dropped their guns. The guns never hit the ground; they instead flew off into the shadows.

"Very good," said the voice. "Now leave."

The two men let out a short cry as they were dropped to the ground. They picked themselves up, looked toward the voice, then toward each other. As if in silent agreement, the men turned and ran.

There was a crunching sound along the dirt path, the sound of approaching footsteps. After a brief moment, an orange tabby and a Russian Blue emerged from the shadows, tales waving triumphant in the air. A man and a teenage boy followed behind them.

"I dare say, your friend Logan does not seem to

like you very much," said the teenager, walking toward Alistair with a casual, yet confident swagger. He had a pronounced British accent, his diction clipped and polished. It was the voice of someone who had clearly attended the finest schools in England. A cocky smile spread across the teenager's face.

Alistair found himself staring at the teenager in spite of himself. He was thin and lanky with caramel skin and exotic dark eyes. He wore a well-tailored, linen, Italian sports jacket, the color of heavy cream. Under the jacket, his designer, camel-colored matching shirt and pants were only a few shades darker than his skin. He was not wearing the type of clothes one would expect to see on a teenager. They were far too sophisticated and expensive. The kid looked like a supermodel and had the mannerisms of a rock star.

"Logan's not a friend. He's an obsessed competitor," replied Alistair.

There was something else about the kid, something familiar. Alarms were going off in his head, and he knew for some reason this teenager's identity was important. With the force of a tsunami, the memory returned. He had seen that face on a bust, one of the only existing representations of the pharaoh himself.

No! That's not possible!

There was a short, frightened whimper. Alistair turned his head, following the desperate cry. It came from the man who had accompanied the teenager. The man was short, overweight, and sweaty. He looked at the teenager with fear and apprehension. That was when Alistair saw it. The man held the Egyptian statue in his right hand; the statue that had brought him to this place.

"Hey! That's my statue!" he yelled.

"Well, not quite," said the teenager. "As I was about to say—"

"It is him!" exclaimed the man in an Arabic accent. Alistair now recognized the man as his contact, Sahid. "It is the Dark Pharaoh himself! It is the mummy!"

The teenager smiled with an almost feline satisfaction at the recognition.

"This is your business partner, is it not?" asked the Dark Pharaoh, looking up at Sahid.

Sahid looked nervous and gave a short nod.

"Sahid here was almost intercepted by one of Logan's men about a half a block away." The two cats jumped up on a low wall next to him as he spoke. "I couldn't simply stand by and let that happen."

Sahid bowed low and extended his arms, offering the statue to the pharaoh. "Your highness, I meant no disrespect. Please take the statue and return to your tomb. I have many small children who depend on me to survive. Please allow me to live!"

The Dark Pharaoh smiled. "I wouldn't presume to detain you a second longer than necessary. Nonetheless, you went to so much trouble...borrowing, this statue from the Beijing Museum, that I wanted to make sure you were paid first. Mr. Black, do you mind?"

Alistair stared at him. "Huh?"

"Pay the gentleman, please. You brought the money, yes?"

Alistair nodded. He turned and walked over to a stack of boards. He reached behind the stack and pulled out a briefcase. He walked back and handed the briefcase to Sahid in return for the statue. The two stared at each other, then turned and stared at the pharaoh.

At first, the Dark Pharaoh smiled back at them, but as the stare continued for an uncomfortable period of time, he sighed. "Here's a thought. Sahid, open the briefcase and make sure the money is what was agreed upon. Alistair, please examine the statue. Is this what you were expecting? Come on gentleman, this is a business transaction."

Sahid opened the brief case and Alistair carefully checked the statue for the telltale signs of an authentic piece.

After a moment, the Dark Pharaoh asked. "Well, is everyone happy?"

The two nodded.

"Excellent! Sahid, you have your money, so you are free to go home to—"

Without a word, Sahid darted back down the path toward the street.

"Oh, and yes, you are very welcome!" the Pharaoh called out after him.

As the frightened man disappeared into the dark, the Dark Pharaoh turned to Alistair and sighed. "Good manners are so lacking these days."

"Yeah, well, that's my take away from all of this, too," mumbled Alistair.

After a brief pause, the Pharaoh began to rub his hands together and said, "So. The statue. We have the next clue. Very exciting! What does it say? Where do we go next?"

"We?"

"Well, yes, I figured you wouldn't mind. You see, it just so happens that I also have a desperate need to return to the tomb myself. Long story, but it is of absolutely no concern of yours. My word of honor, you can have all the treasures in the tomb. I don't really care about any of that. I just need… something else in there. Of minor importance, really. You don't mind, do you? I was, after all, of considerable help to you tonight. Someone of my talents could prove to be invaluable in this sort of quest. Yes?"

"You want to…," stumbled Alistair. He shook his head and stared hard at him. "Are you…nuts?"

The Dark Pharaoh looked taken aback. "No, I simply can't recall how to get back to the tomb. I left that place a few thousand years ago and everything in Egypt has changed so much. You know how it is. I need a little help, that's all. I'm proposing a partnership. A perfectly fair partnership where we both get we want."

"Uh...no," blurted out Alistair.

"Oh. You want money? Oh, of course you do. You're a professional. You deserve to be compensated. How much? I'm sure we can work something out." The Dark Pharaoh smiled confidently.

Alistair couldn't seem to get the words out and instead started shaking his head.

The Pharaoh's smile fell abruptly. "You're saying no. Really? I must say, I can't quite wrap my brain around it. I saved your life. I saved Sahid and the statue. Can we at least talk about it? Discuss it like two civilized human beings, yes?"

Silence. Alistair was still in shock and couldn't seem to say the obvious truth.

"Is it because you think I'm an impostor?"

"No, I saw your bust in the British museum during my research. I saw your powers, throwing those guys around. Saying it now, it all sounds insane, but in light of the evidence, yes, I actually do believe you're the Dark Pharaoh."

"Well, then...why? I don't understand—"

"Because you're the freakin' mummy of the tomb!" yelled the archaeologist, far louder than he intended. "You should be my enemy on this, trying to stop me! I'm planning on breaking into your tomb. You should be threatening to put curses on me, killing people, crashing about!"

The Pharaoh looked startled. "Good heavens,

that wouldn't be very civilized. Besides, all that silliness with the tomb, it was so long ago. Why would I care about any of that stuff now? It's not like it's really my tomb, after all. I'm an immortal. I was never even in it."

There was another long, awkward pause.

The Dark Pharaoh's face brightened. "You know, I haven't properly introduced you to my cats. How rude of me!"

"Uh, I don't think that's really important right now."

"This is—" he started to say as he reached out his hand to touch the gray cat, but she hissed at him and he jerked his hand away just in time to miss being hit with a vicious claw. "Well, then."

He smiled a little and said, "Her dinner is a little late. Makes her grumpy. Her name is Reptile."

"What kind of name is Reptile?" questioned Alistair.

Could this night get any weirder? he thought.

"Well, once you get to know her, you'll understand."

"Uh-huh," mumbled Alistair, not sure what else to say.

"And this is Nicky," he said, patting the orange cat on the head. The cat smiled and looked exceedingly happy.

Reptile, seeing that Nicky was getting all the attention, pushed her head under the Pharaoh's hand until he finally began petting her. She started purring.

"So, back on topic. You won't work with me because you think I will harm you or possibly others? And if I gave you my word of honor that I will not harm anyone except in the defense of others or myself, that would not sway you?"

"Well, you seem pleasant enough," admitted the archaeologist. "It's just...if this was a mummy movie, which it seems to be, you're the monster, so I can't trust you."

The pharaoh's face abruptly darkened with anger. "I'm the what? The monster? I beg your pardon?"

"Well...uh..." Alistair said.

The pharaoh began to pace back and forth. "Really! I'm the monster? Me? After all I've been through the last few years and I'm stuck with the label of 'monster'!? No, that is unacceptable. They can force everything else on me, but not...I am not the monster here!"

The pharaoh stopped pacing and turned to look at Alistair. His eyes narrowed thoughtfully.

"Come with me. It's time that I took you backstage of this so-called movie and introduced you to the real monster." He then ran back down the dirt path toward the street, his cats in hot pursuit.

Alistair, was left dumbstruck. An angry mummy on the rampage was the kind of trouble he had feared moments ago and now that seemed to be exactly what he had triggered with his accusation. He began to limp quickly down the path.

Alistair was about 20 feet behind when the Dark Pharaoh entered the street. A black van was pulling away from the curb and started to speed away. It had only traveled a few yards when the pharaoh made a motion with his hands. The van rose into the air, spun three times and then dropped to the ground, landing right side up.

"Hey!" yelled Alistair, catching up to the furious pharaoh who was marching toward the van. "What the hell are you doing?!"

"Don't go into hysterics, they're fine." The Pharaoh grasped the handle of the sliding door. "Besides, every last one of them deserves far worse, believe me."

With a metallic snap, which Alistair assumed was the sound of the door lock breaking, the Pharaoh jerked open the door.

"Hello," the Pharaoh said in a prim and proper voice to the terrified looking man who was lying on the floor of the van. "Remember me? I need a few things from you, do you mind?"

Before the man could answer, the Pharaoh grabbed him by the collar and with his free hand jerked a small black wallet out of the man's jacket pocket. He then threw the man roughly out of the van and tossed the wallet to Alistair. Afterwards, he climbed into the van and began punching buttons on a device in the cargo area. Alistair looked down at the wallet and opened it to find a badge inside. The initials were not familiar, "FDSO." However, the words printed at the top, were very familiar. They read: "United States of America."

"FDSO: Federal Department of Security Operations," said the Dark Pharaoh. "Or as I like to call them, the Fucking Dumb Shit Ops. They work for the American government. They're like the NSC and CIA and the rest of that alphabet soup, but their job is a little unusual. Their job is to control people like me."

"There are other people out there like you?" asked the archaeologist, stunned.

The pharaoh smiled. "People who are different, but whose existence isn't common knowledge. Vampires and werewolves fall under their control as well."

The pharaoh hit a button on the device, and Alistair heard a recording of his own voice played back. "If this was a horror movie, you'd be the monster!"

The pharaoh slammed the stop button and turned to glare at the archaeologist.

"Well, this isn't a movie, this is reality. And the reality of our situation is that the United States government is the real monster! Or should I say, one of the monsters. Either way, they are the reason I'm here. They are holding my two daughters hostage! If I don't come back with the immortality serum that's locked in that tomb, they're going to..."

His voice trailed off in a choked sob.

Another car screeched to a stop next to the van and four men climbed out, pulled out their guns and pointed them at the pharaoh and Alistair.

"Get out of our van, *thing*," the lead man said.

The Dark Pharaoh huffed and threw a glance at Alistair. The lead man stepped closer to the pharaoh, pushing the gun into his face. "Do what I say or you know what they will do to your daughters!"

Alistair looked at the man, stunned. No denial of the accusation that they were going to harm his daughters, and no pity either. The Dark Pharaoh was telling the truth.

The pharaoh stepped out of the van and with the gun still pointed in his face said "One little correction to that statement, Mr. Rutherford. If I don't come back with the immortality serum, my daughters will be harmed. If I kill you, however," he said, taking a step toward Mr. Rutherford. Neither flinched and their noses were nearly touching. "The circumstances are quite different, aren't they? I could kill you, your men, pop your collective heads off your necks like bottle caps, and your superiors will do absolutely nothing other than replace you. Because my assignment is to bring back the serum, nothing more. And to put it very simply, you and your men are nothing but tools to an end. I may be a thing, a monster, in the eyes of your agency, but you hold no more value to your superiors than a disposable pen."

Some of the other men exchanged glances, clearly hitting it the mark with them. Rutherford's eyes remained locked onto the pharaoh with a cold, penetrating stare.

"You may have some telekinetic powers, but against all of our weapons and all of our technology, we will win every single time," said Mr. Rutherford. "Kill me and my men if you want, but you are still FDSO's bitch. Now get us that serum!"

He then turned to Alistair and said, "Mr. Black, I strongly recommend that you assist Mr. Osiris."

Osiris? thought Alistair. *That was the god of the underworld. Why is he calling him that?*

"As far as we are concerned, you're in as deep as this guy. Find the serum or you might just find yourself on the other end of a particularly nasty tax audit. Then let's see how well you conduct your future archaeological digs from a prison cell."

The government agents climbed back into their respective vehicles and sped away. The pharaoh stared after them, his expression of defiance slowly fading. Now he seemed somehow smaller, deflated. He walked past Alistair, toward the two cats who were sitting on the curb across the street. He sat down on the curb next to them and they crawled into his lap.

"Osiris?" asked Alistair.

"Yes. Osiris. I named myself after the God of the Underworld." He smiled mirthlessly. "You see, my entire life I was obsessed with achieving immortality, cheating death. Then one of my priests actually figured it out. I insisted that I be referred to as Osiris, saying that since I cheated death, I therefore had stolen his crown and now was the true God of the Underworld."

"Bet that went over well," said Alistair.

Osiris laughed. "Oh, yes. Very. There was an uprising among the priests. Can't blame them. They were afraid they would incur the wrath of the true god Osiris, after all. So I ended up fleeing for my life and didn't stop running until I hit Ethiopia. Saying my name was forbidden, which is how I ended up being the Dark Pharaoh with no name. Well, I say screw them. They're all dead and I'm still around using the name Osiris. I say the best revenge is outliving your enemies by several thousand years or more."

"And you think the serum is in your tomb?"

"I instructed the priest to put it there. He was a loyal man. And I have never run across any other immortals, so I don't believe he sold it to anyone. To the best of my knowledge, my daughters and I are the only immortals. Not counting vampires and werewolves, of course." He saw the question in Alistair's eyes and added. "The serum must have altered my genes somehow. They're immortal too."

"But if they're immortal, those agents can't kill them, right?"

Osiris looked at him with a stunned expression on his face. "Meaning what? That they're safe? My good man, think about it. If they can't get the serum from a bottle, then they'll dissect my daughters to get it. Imagine what that would be like. Being strapped down to a table, dissected alive and probably fully conscious, because heaven knows they wouldn't want to give them pain killers that might mask the test results. And there my girls would be, day after day, enduring one medical experiment after another, without even the hope of death to end their pain. It's...unimaginable."

"My God! They would do that!?"

"Of course. We're just things, creatures in their minds. Why wouldn't they?"

"I guess you're right about not being the monster in this picture," muttered Alistair. "I can't believe the United States government would do something like this. Does the president know?"

"What difference does it make?" grumbled Osiris. "Whether it is a government-sanctioned action or a rogue agency, all that matters is getting my daughters back!"

Alistair started to pace, trying to clear his mind. There had to be something they could do, some angle they could play.

He stopped abruptly. "You said there was another monster?"

Osiris nodded. "Logan is working for the other monster, a pharmaceutical company."

Alistair nodded. "Of course they would want the serum. The money they could make selling an immortality drug—"

Osiris broke out in a fit of laughter.

"What? What's so funny?"

"Are you insane?" Osiris finally blurted out. "They want to destroy the serum! No more sick people, no more money!"

Alistair stared at Osiris dumbfounded. A disheartening thought, but he couldn't argue with the man's logic.

Alistair thought about the expedition he had originally planned, and how radically different it had turned out. Here his greatest hope was to find the tomb, but instead he was now paired with an Egyptian Pharaoh. A real live Pharaoh! Instead of guessing at the past, he could actually talk to this guy, learn the real truth. His eyes moved down to his artificial leg. He had just about decided to give it all up, retire. And now he had made the greatest archaeological discovery of all time without ever leaving Jersey. There was no way in hell he was going to retire now.

As if he could hear Alistair's thoughts, Osiris turned to him and said in a cheerful voice. "Well, so enough with the introductions. Shall we begin our adventure?"

THE FULL MOON EXPRESS

BY: JONATHAN MOON

Typically, long-haul truck drivers try their best to avoid treacherous high mountain roads like the one snaking between Falterwood and Stillwater. The turns are sharp and frequent and, even from the high vantage point of an eighteen wheeler, often blind. Rolling yet surprisingly sharp the road snaps to the left and right, a nation's worth of rural 'Deadman's Curves' crammed into a forty mile stretch of road. Paved side-roads crisscross and spider web the dense terrain leading to hidden private residences and secluded local businesses. The tall pines lining the epileptic curvy road give the false sense of safety from the suns blinding rays while they themselves blur together as motorists pass, forming disorienting walls of forest famous for confusing drivers. Driveways and patchy logging roads meet the main road, Hoo-Doo Lane, at corners and bends, navigated wildly by the locals that grew up on them, adding reckless metal death machines to the already lethal mix.

Too many old timers have seen the tangled smoking messes and told the tales of them with pale faces and wet eyes enunciating their terror. Since the founding of the two small cities on opposite ends of a rugged mountain range, and the few smaller towns and villages hidden between, the road has gained a reputation that keeps only the most seasoned drivers supplying the towns with their needs and goods despite the fear sweat that stains their shirts and the years each close call shaves from a meth-fueled heart. Even those that made their livings on the road between Stillwater and Falterwood feared it every time they rode it.

Save for Leon. He cruises his big silver 1995 Kenworth W900L (Cat 3406E engine, 435 horse, and tight as gnat-ass 13 speeds), with its proud name 'The Full Moon Express' emblazoned across its doors, down every snaking road between the two mountain burgs with a smile on his face. One would never realize as much because Leon's ravenous grin is always obscured by his thick black beard. Leon has driven longer routes in his time, crossing the consumerist nation on its flat sleeping-pill highways as an ever-spinning cog in the supply and demand machine, but now he prefers the treacherous high mountain loop. He has always found it to be the perfect road for picking-up his victims/ forbidden meals.

Leon used to live in Lincoln, North Dakota and drive a route from Bismarck to Tacoma, Washington under the employ of a company that sold polyethylene beads to factories which melted them into gas and water lines. He would pick up hitchhikers with a sincere smile on his beardless face and he'd savor every cut and thrust as he raped and killed scores of forgotten children across the North West. Leon kept one pallet of black polyethylene beads in his trailer at all times, and swimming in those beads wrapped tight in plastic were his decaying trophies. He drew a smiley face on the cardboard lid with red permanent marker to insure it was never inadvertently delivered to any of the stops along his route. The voice in his head, his *Urge*, has guided him from birth; each swipe of the blade and careful move to cover his ass has been spoken in the gravelly voice of his psychopathic bloodlust.

Since his change three years ago Leon doesn't drive for any outfit other than himself and he doesn't deliver goods (unless you count half-devoured corpses dumped in hidden hard-to-hike gulches and fern-obscured creeks). At a truckstop outside of Spokane Leon got bit by a little feral looking bitch right on his member the split second before he drove an ice-pick clean through her skull. He wrapped his bit trout in gauze and dumped her carcass in a ditch lit by the lights from a tribal casino. With the rise of the full moon two nights later Leon had a new power along with a new hunger and a new voice, the ***Beast***. He became a werewolf and the lycanthropy tainting his blood became another homicidal master.

Gone is the pallet-mounted box of beads stuffed with rotting dismembered chunks of past conquests. At the behest of the Beast the trailer is lined with wooden boxes made to keep prey for the nights the Beast takes form, controlling both mind and body while shoving Leon's mind deep into the small bloody room his Urge resides in. While the Beast lies physically dormant the lingering effects of the change still show; a slight restructuring of his facial bones, thick dark facial and body hair, sharp enlarged canine teeth and finger nails, as well as extra muscle mass and canine quick reflexes. Leon and his Urge take full advantage of his new traits and use them as he tortures and rapes his prey, be they male or female, until the Beast awakens to feast on them. It always amazes Leon how they all scream when he transforms into the totality of the Beast. Eyes clouded over with acceptance of their slow tortuous end suddenly blink to quivering life in the face of the six-inch canine teeth and the terrible promise of painful death they bring. The Urge must be careful, however, not to push too far and kill the prey as the Beast won't eat dead meat and if it doesn't have prey trapped and waiting it would go on the hunt. And the hunt was a savage and reckless thing, capable of undoing all of Leon's self-taught pre-cautions while he lies huddled, helpless, within his bestial form.

Right now, Leon and his Urge face that very dilemma; the trailer rattling behind is empty of fleshy cargo. It has been for the past week. Since Leon's long slender fingers flipped the plastic latches on his brand new six-piece industrial pruning set and the Urge knew it would go too far and play too rough. And it did. A recently retired couple had been waiting for the Beast but they were no match for the six-piece tool set in the hands of a master of brutal artistic dementia such as the Urge. Even though two of the six pieces are counted as the molded plastic carrying case and the holster for the pruners, the pruners themselves, the lopper, the shears, and the folding ten inch saw all were over-effective in their new applications. The Urge, dizzy with satisfaction, ordered Leon to a secluded creek where they dropped the shredded corpses amongst the ferns before going about their day as if nothing had happened.

As the sun hangs fat and low in the sky, floating just above the tree tops, the monsters inside of Leon are getting hungry. Leon hears them in his head. The *Urge* is confident and cold and depraved while the ***Beast*** is commanding and selfish and primal.

Nearly sunset! I hunger!

The Beast has said nothing else besides announcing its hunger for the entirety of the day. Leon has made the round trip three times today, gassed up twice and still has found nothing to silence the Beast. As he pulls The Full Moon Express out of Stillwater for the third time of the day he catches a glimpse of a blond woman fifty feet ahead with her thumb out. He smiles under his tangled beard and tugs his bright yellow truckers cap, a faded remembrance from his first post-Beast kill, down his shield his eyes. The feisty looking cartoon beaver crammed between the words Falterwood and Beavers on his cap scowls down at the girl with splotchy crimson buck-teeth that nearly match Leon's red and yellow flannel.

Her! I'll have my feast!

And there is still enough time for me to have a moment of fun.

Her hair looks soft and wild, more wavy than curvy, as it hangs down to her breasts. She wears a bright yellow tank-top and a bright colored paisley sundress that stands out against the earthy forest tones behind her like an acid trip in a cave. Leon's enhanced vision drags from her out stretched thumb, up the contours of her thin-but muscled-arms, over the smoothness of her exposed neck where he almost sees the artery pumping sweet hot blood, to her slender face and blonde hair before amusing his Urge and dropping his eyes over her pert breasts pressing against the yellow fabric and the sundress as it sticks to the blonde's shapely legs and crotch like a colorfully patterned second skin.

She'll be fun to play with.

She will make a sweet feast!

With his homicidal inner-voices in agreement, Leon slows the truck using his engine break more for show than necessity. The blond steps back to allow extra room for the massive rig, until the branches from the vibrant green bushes behind her bend and yield to her and her bright clothes. Leon's keen eyes see branches scratch the tanned flesh of her shoulder leaving bright red scrapes not angry enough to break her skin. Leon grinds to a halt right in front of her so she has a clear view of the gaudy 'The Full Moon Express' custom made decals. Leon watches her shiver, ever so slightly, and he sees the fear cloud her face for only a split second before fading into the darkness behind her leaving only a slight twitch at the corners of her smile as the only sign of its existence. As fleeting as the flush of fear was both of Leon's monsters saw it, they breathed it in faint as perfume in a landfill, and it tempted them.

Oh sweet fear. ***Sweet flesh!***

Leon sets the brake and scoots to the edge of his custom bucket seat. He leans across the matching passenger seat and smiles down as he unlocks the door for the blonde. She steps even further into the brush to allow the door room enough to swing before she catches it. A rush of strange smells assault Leon's senses just as he sees a dark blur in the trees behind the girl. An instant later a clean shaven man in a Chicago Bears hoodie and his face half hidden under Aviator sunglasses darts out of the trees, past the blonde and right up into the cab of the Full Moon Express where he settles in between the two bucket seats. The blonde follows right behind him and a second man, this one wearing an army surplus camouflage jacket and with shaggy black hair, emerges as she climbs in. The last man in scoots underneath the blonde as her ass hovers in midair above the seat. She settles in his lap and smiles sheepishly at Leon.

They will ruin everything! Kill them now, Leon!
No! It will be a feast!

Leon hears the monsters in his head clearly but bellows his own thought, "What the hell?"

"Hey, thanks for picking us up, mister," the blonde says ignoring his shouted question as if she hadn't even heard him. "We must have been standing there for close to three hours waiting for a ride. So many cars speed by, but nobody stops and picks people up any more. Too many psychos with their raping and robbing and killing their way around the nation, I guess. It sure was sweet of you, mister."

Leon studies the smoothness of her skin and the paleness of her blues eyes, the desire to carve his name in her cheeks with a box knife while he chews on her squishy salty orb nearly over whelms him. His breaths are deep and guttural as he watches her pink slightly wind-chapped lips as she talks.

"Yeah, three hours, mister, then Declan and I duck into the woods for thirty seconds to take a piss and Megan scores us a right comfortable ride in no time flat. Thanks for the ride, mister." The man under Megan adds. Dark hair frames his handsome but unsmiling face. Both his eyes and voice are cold-the cold of a killer, both a warning and a threat, but Leon is impossible to scare.

The burly werewolf sociopath trucker has survived death several times since becoming the Beast, tragedies befalling him both as wolf and as (mad) man, yet no matter how terrible and messy each death has been his body had miraculously eventually healed itself. The degree of injury affects the time the regeneration takes. When a half-skinned hooker buried his own wood-working awl deep into his windpipe with a lucky last-breath rally for revenge he collapsed in the corner of the cargo bed, choking on his blood and sucking in more air from the new ragged hole in his throat than his mouth. His world grew black slowly, The Urge was surprisingly silent though out, offering no words of regret or comfort while Leon watched his unlikely killer fade away into the blackness first. He awoke an hour later, his throat raw and hot and his prick fully erect, and he whistled while he finished skinning the hooker with the lucky aim.

But when, on a full moon chase after escaping prey the focused Beast scampered across the highway and was smashed flat by a speeding WankCo

Supply Company delivery truck it took nearly three days before his body had dragged itself back together enough for him to move. Leon was vaguely aware of everything those long tortuous three days lying splattered across the road- the pain as raw nerves scraped across hot asphalt and the sun stealing all the moisture from his sinewy chunks as they inched slowly together. His thoughts were simple and focused as drying chunks of himself crept and crawled across the blacktop, fusing to other chunks as it moved unnaturally towards the same spot hidden behind bushes on the side of the road. When he awoke he hurt all over like he had taken a kazoo to a baseball bat fight. He vomited where he laid and then, naked as the day he was born, crawled two miles back to the Full Moon Express where he slept another two days for good measure.

A cold tone from a cock-strong punk didn't scare Leon even a little bit. "I wasn't picking you all up," he grumbles while shifting the big rig back into gear.

"That's not creepy. Not at all." Declan says from where he crouches next to Leon. His eyes are hidden behind his wide reflective lens of his sunglasses but the smile on his face appears far friendlier than the one his companion wears. Leon sniffs the myriad of new aromas the three strangers wafted in with them. He smells gun powder, from at least two guns, and sweat, cold sweat born of determination, not fear or heat. He tastes the tang of Megan's arousal, the sour of the Declan's day-old beer breath, and the sweetness of their adrenaline-charged blood rushing through their hearts and bodies. He grunts at the still smiling Declan as he pulls back onto the road.

Armed and arrogant, they should die now, before they try something. ***I will feast first!***

Leon considers the growling voices in his head while the three strangers adjust to the stiffness of the ride as it rumbles down the black top. Before the silence has time to become uncomfortable Megan tells Leon, "My name is Megan. This cute fella acting as my car seat is my boyfriend, Jed. And the charmer next to you is Declan."

Leon takes his eyes off the looming curve ahead and looks the three over with a grunt. "I'm Leon."

I will gorge on all this flesh! Render flesh from bone! Drown myself in warm sticky blood!

We still have thirty minutes until sunset. There is still time for us to play a little. Some relief to the stress of the day.

We will find more tomorrow. Earlier. These are mine! My feast!

We still have at least thirty minutes.

I won't eat the dead meat. We drive till sunset and then I feast!

Declan smiles at Leon as he sits back and makes himself comfortable. He slides his Aviators down and whistles at the purple imitation silk sheet hanging as a barrier between cab and sleeping quarters.

Leon takes his eyes off the road and gives Declan a quick grimace he hopes relays the throat-ripping rage he is feeling. Declan just keeps smiling. He moves his hand slowly, like a cobra's dance, in front of the purple sheet and it dances in the wind he creates.

"Not the color I would expect from a rugged fella like you, Leon." Declan jokes. Megan and Jed both chuckle.

Now they tease. They are begging for it. ***NO! They are mine!***

Leon doesn't take his eyes off the road or respond with words. Instead he swallows hard and loud. The sound is guttural and rude; Megan winces, Jed shifts uncomfortably under her weight, and Declan acts as if he didn't hear anything- so entranced in the purple sheets waving in rhythm with his fingers. When Jed shifts Megan wagers a look out the window. The trees blur past, tall columns of wood strengthening the vast cities of shadow within them, and Megan recoils from the window and its view. She takes a deep silent breath, trying to ground out her panic and play it cool but Leon caught the unmistakable whiff of her fear in the air.

Sweet fear! Sweet pain! ***Sweet feasting!***

Leon steals glances at Megan as he navigates a near-impossible corner. A smile creases his mouth making his beard twitch in response. Her fear warms Leon's blood and makes his tongue swell.

"Hey. Mister, I was asking you about these pretty sheets." Declan reminds Leon with the slightest pang of menace.

They are going to try something. And they are going to try it soon. ***Do not kill them! They are mine! The sun is setting soon!*** *Not soon enough.*

"I heard you," Leon answers while still looking back and forth between the road and Megan, "I was ignoring you. I don't care what kinda shit dazzles you, inside or outside my truck." Leon's chest rumbles with another deep rude grunt. "And I told you once my name is Leon."

Stop! They are my feast! *Leon likes me better. He wants what I want.* ***I will feast tonight!***

Leon agrees with the Urge, his old friend and master. Leon has flensed punks like these three and poured used milk jugs full of piss or diesel fuel over them but now, when the full moon looms, the Beast dictates the kill. His tone doesn't mask his irritation.

Unfazed, Declan shrugs and makes his fingers a gun which he then shoots Leon with accompanying 'kitch-kitch' noises. Leon is already ignoring him again so Declan goes back to fanning the purple silky wall.

Leon asks Megan, "You okay, Miss? First time in a big rig?"

Megan sighs, relieved to not have to hide her apprehensions any longer, "I've been in them before. They scare the living shit out of me, to tell ya the truth."

She laughs nervously. No one joins in and she stops quickly, her face flashing through two shades of sudden embarrassment. Then she blurts, "And werewolves."

Declan and Jed both point and laugh at Megan like drunken frat kids. They both tease her while she tells them both to shut up. Leon barely hears their words over the voices in his head.

She fears me! You will feel her fear for me! *I want her to fear me!* ***She will.*** *Not the obvious horror that accompanies your glowing eyes and gnashing fucking teeth! I want her to see me in Leon's eyes and know I'm cutting her fingers off cute little digit by cute little digit.* ***I'll taste the meat and you can have the fear and pain!*** *I want it to quell it from her myself!*

Leon speaks over the continued snickered comments from Jed and Declan and the murderous voices in his head, "That's all terrible, Miss, but I'm a hell of a driver and I'll keep ya safe."

"Ain't you just a sweetheart, Leon?" Jed asks in a cold mocking tone.

Declan joins right in, like a kid following a bully from nerd to nerd, "I could tell from the moment I saw these glorious sheets!"

They still tease! ***We will have our revenge as scraps of their flesh dangle from our jaws!*** *Now! We kill them now!* ***NO! The sun is setting! You can see it and feel it!*** *Now, then, in the waning twilight between sunset and moon rise!* ***NO!***

A growl from deep within Leon's chest rumbles up his throat like a burp. Megan shutters and slaps Jed's shoulder. "Stop it, the both of you. Leon was kind enough to give us a ride."

The smiles on Jed and Declan's faces melt into the scowls of scolded children. Without their grins they both seem much more dangerous. Leon feels their anger against his cheek like the rays of a hateful sun. Leon ignores them and tells Megan, "Thanks, Miss, I wasn't picking them up."

Megan's nervous grin evaporates and the real cold bitch beneath shines through. She raises her voice to a tone implying threat but not danger, "Okay, I get it, Leon. And I told you once my name is Megan not Miss."

Jed suppresses his laughter with a snort. The dark hairs on the back of Leon's neck stand on end electrified by the tense anger-charged mood in the cab. He smells Megan's arousal, a musk every bit as sensual as her fear. Leon smells Jed's testosterone as it floods his system. Leon hears the young man's muscles tighten all the way across the cab. Leon looks Megan in her angry eyes and smiles wide enough for her to see the elongated canine teeth. The quick grin dissolves into Leon's beard and he mumbles, "Sorry, Miss", as he turns back to the road.

Declan is still waving his hand in front of the billowing sheets and watching them dance, seemingly unfazed by the tense mood around him. "I'm sorry I teased ya, Leon. I like these."

Leon grunts at Declan but doesn't respond further. The silence which follows sings inside the cab along with the hum of the road outside while the tension dances to the song. Jed and Megan are trying to have a conversation with their eyes. Leon watches them out of the corner of his. He starts salivating into his beard.

Declan waves his hand closer to the curtain and it sinks away from his hand far enough he sees something on the floor of Leon's sleeping quarters. He holds his breath as he slowly pulls a Mossberg 12 gauge shotgun all the way into his lap. Jed and Megan both jump back a little when Leon leans over lazily and smiles fondly at the shotgun in Declan's hands.

"Nice hardware, Leon!" Declan nearly shouts in an excited kid-in-the-candy-store voice.

What little skin on Leon's face not obscured by his beard blushes bright red. Leon is not used to conversation with other people, much less compliments. He usually only hears pleas and promises and threats and screams and moans and prayers. His first instinct is to tell Declan how it had a hand that ended in a bloody stump gripped tight to it when he first acquired it. He doesn't need the monsters inside of him to know not to.

Declan runs his fingers up the smoothness of the barrel, then, pulls them back when they rub over deep gouges in the steel which bur up the metal into razor sharp ridges. He looks at his bleeding fingers, three small but deep cuts trisecting the pad of his index finger. He stuffs it in his mouth and sucks the blood away but not before Leon inhales the scent of it. Leon's head swoons, his adrenaline pumping so fast he is turning junkie-pale.

"Damn, is this police issue?" Declan asks.

"Yup." Leon answers without looking at him.

"Did you find it after an accident or something? Is it black market? Why is it so scuffed up?" Declan's questions come rapid fire with no time for answers in between.

"You sure got a lot of questions," Leon mumbles.

"Just one more," Declan says as he points the shotgun at Leon, "is it loaded?"

Leon smirks. Quicker than humanly possible he reaches over and snatches the gun from Declan's startled hands. He lays the gun gently on the other side of his seat and says, "Yup."

"Enough!" Megan shouts and Jed pulls a .45 Glock 36 out of the folds of his camouflage jacket. He trains it on Leon's face, his hands the steady hands of a killer. Once Jed has Leon in his sights Declan slowly, almost causally, retrieves his own handgun, an old police issue Smith and Wesson 38 Special Square Butt, and points it at Leon's ear.

I told you. They have done this before. We need to kill them now! ***No. The sun is setting. I will feast in minutes!***

"Pull into the rest stop we're coming up on. It's about ten minutes before we hit junction at the next little shit hole town. Your ride is over, big dog." Jed's voice is cold and confident, his words measured and rehearsed.

"Bentley." Leon says with a nod.

"What?" Jed snaps and straightens his arm so the tip of his gun inches closer to Leon's face.

The Beast begins clawing for release, driven by hunger and impatient with the slow rising moon. Leon chokes down the change the best he can, hoping to reach the rest area before the Beast assumes control. His words are grunted and strained, "the next.. little…shit hole…town…is Bentley."

"What the fuck ever! You aren't going there! You're pulling into the rest area ten minutes before it, got it, big dog?"

"Big…Dog," Leon chuckles to himself as the first glowing edge of the moon peeks up from the pink and yellow horizon. He retches drool, bile, and blood all over himself as his organs begin shifting and stretching. He grips the wheel out of instinct while he curls up and slams himself into his door. The sound of Leon's bones snapping and elongating and his skin splitting and re-growing anew echoes inside the cramped cab. Though his hands are gripping the steering wheel Leon is lost in the agony of the change and the truck and trailer begin to swerve on the narrow mountain road.

"What the hell?" Jed screams, his cold threatening tone lost to his panic and fear.

Declan says nothing while Megan just screams and screams.

Grunts, yelps, and growls are emitting from Leon's hunched form as his hands jerk the steering wheel back and forth. The flesh on the hands bubbles and tears, revealing shiny white bone that splinters before reforming into longer thicker bone quickly covered with new tough black hide and coarse black hair. Long sharp claws sprout from the end of Leon's morphing fingers popping each of his small human fingernails out of their way and dropping them, blood-streaked, to the floor boards.

The three would-be robbers stare at the growling convulsing Leon until the headlights from a car in the other lane grabs their collective attention. The big silver Kenworth swerves across the double yellow line and back whipping the trailer dangerously as it snaps back and forth.

"Do something!" Megan screams over the honking of the oncoming car.

Jed shoves her off his lap into the cramped space between seat and dash board. He reaches bravely for the wheel but recoils when he catches sight of the flesh of Leon's face undergoing the same horrendous change as his hand. Seeing his partner hesitate, Declan dives over Leon's hunched form and grabs the steering wheel. His hands are next to the bubbling stretching claws gripped tight but useless there. He ignores them the best he can as he cranks the wheel hard away from the honking car. The cab swings out of the way without a second to spare, but the torture chamber trailer swings wide and bats the opposing driver and their vehicle off the road. Headlights bounce wildly into the trees where the car is impaled into the trunk of a centuries old cedar. Declan sees the smoking heap of metal nearly hidden by the tall pines surrounding it but focuses on aiming the eighteen wheeler into the quickly approaching rest area.

The Full Moon Express bounces over one small concrete block, slamming it to chalky dust, before narrowly avoiding the larger wall constructed of concrete slabs acting as unforgiving guide into the parking lot. The silver Kenworth rumbles alongside the wall as it loses speed until it finally rolls to a stop a mere twenty feet from the log cabin-looking rest rooms. The semi rattles loudly and spits acrid puffs of black smoke as it dies.

At some point during the chaos Declan's Aviators were flung off his face and he smiles now at Megan and Jed, his green eyes glowing in the twilight, at his luck in stopping the runaway rig. Instead of Megan and Jed returning his relieved grin they grimace at something behind him. Declan remembers the claws forcing the fingernails away with wet popping sounds. Out of the corner of his eye he sees the shotgun Leon grabbed away from him slid up underneath the pedals. He takes a deep measured breath and reaches for it.

Leon has undergone the change. The Beast is in control now.

Feast!

With a soft whistle something moves behind Declan quicker than his mind can follow. In the next blink of his eye, Leon snaps forward and latches onto his shoulder with jaws like a steel trap. Teeth tear through flesh with ease, shredding muscle as they sink into bone. Blood splashes across Declan's face and he gurgles a scream.

Jed and Megan are frozen with fear watching the werewolf gnaw on Declan's shoulder. Its fur is the same coarse black of Leon's beard and its moose-sized face is shaped like a wolf bred in hell. Its red eyes glow like iridescent coals fanned with hunger and stoked with fury. The Beast grinds its massive jaws, tearing through the sinew, muscle and cartilage that was Declan's shoulder. Another splash of blood born from Declan's gaping wound sprays everyone in the cab eliciting a fresh chorus of screams.

"Keeee-rist!" Jed bellows as he fires the .45 at the Beast. The first shot is high and buries itself into the ceiling. The second bullet takes the Beast's right ear off with a puff of smoke and blood.

The Beast roars in irritated pain though the sound is muffled by the shoulder in its maw. It responds by giving Declan a violent shake, sinking its teeth even deeper still, as Megan reaches for the door handle. The door opens, its squeak muffled by the ringing in everyone's ears from the gunfire in the confined space, and Megan falls to the ground. She crawls a few feet before gaining her footing. Jed fires a third shot, which bounces off the rhino-hard skin of the Beast's shoulder and ricochets into the driver's seat with a sizzle. He drops out behind Megan, falling on his ass and firing the forth shot (a second into the cab ceiling) from there before rolling to his feet and following Megan into the woods.

Declan watches his friends flee before his vision blurs, takes on a sharp red tint, and then fades into blackness. The Beast tears greedily at his unconscious prize, birthing warm spurts of crimson blood with every tug. It doesn't rip away any flesh yet; it tenderizes first.

From deep in the mental prison the Urge is confined to during the Beast's hours Leon's first monster growls at the Beast, *Two other are fleeing.*

I am feasting. Leave me be!

We have to kill them. WE can't let them escape while YOU feed so greedily!

The musk of Declan's blood dizzies the Beast with ravenous hunger that consumes the entirety of its primal thoughts. Yet, it has learned, as Leon has, its best to not ignore the irritating voice of the Urge. Over the sound of shredding muscles The Beast hears noises beyond the cab of the truck. It ceases its chewing and listens. The Beast hears their foot falls as they run from the edge of the parking lot blacktop into the darkened forest beyond. It hears their ragged frightened breathing. It hears Jed mumbling curses. It hears Megan crying.

The Beast snarls viciously through its mouthful of meat, simultaneously furious and exhilarated about the forced hunt to come. The Beast releases it death-grip on Declan and lets the chewed man slowly drop from its jaws. A growl, a blur, and the Beast is out of the truck sniffing for his fleeing prey. The hell borne Beast stalks the parking lot searching for the path its prey had chosen through the tangle of vast evergreens. The newly risen moon casts its glow down upon the horrible Beast bringing its hellish features into greater detail. Dark coarse hair covers the ten foot Beast's head, face, chest, belly, wrist and ankles. Where dark fur does not cover the Beast's hide the flesh is as black as it is dense and tough, a supernatural armor never fully hinted at by legend. It moves faster than man or wolf, a dark blur reeking of blood and death, as it finds the path Jed and Megan crashed through the forest. It bays at the fat full moon, a sound that chills the blood of its prey, as it darts into the trees. It grabs wide trunks with its massive clawed hands and uses them to propel itself even faster into the thick of the forest.

Megan can hear the snarling Beast approaching quicker than she can run. She wagers a look behind her at the cost of stubbing her toe into a half buried root and falling face first into the pine needle covered mud. As she hits the ground the Beast slashes its deadly claws where she was just running. She hears the primal whistle as the claws slash empty air and the Beast's resulting growl of frustration but the Beast moves too fast through the dark for her to see.

Jed hears Megan trip and he stops running. He can't hear anything over the thundering of his heart and he can't see anything in the thick wooded metropolis of shadows. He feels rank blood-tinged air sweep across his face as the Beast circles him, toying with him before the inevitable kill. He stumbles forward while firing the .45 randomly into the darkness surrounding him.

Megan sees Jed, his face pale and frightened, in each muzzle flash of his gun. She also sees the Beast, closer to Jed with each flash. Megan is too scared to warn her doomed boyfriend as she pisses herself and scoots away on her ass as quickly and quietly as she can. Jed's gun clicks empty as he steps into a beam of moonlight slicing its way through the dense suffocating darkness. Jed blinks his eyes, blinded by the Beast's maternal moon, just as the Beast emerges slowly from the shadows behind him.

Megan watches through blurry eyes as the Beast grabs Jed by his muscled arms, sinking its stretched claws into the biceps she had been so attracted too. Jed turns to look at the harbinger of his fate but he only sees blood stained teeth before they sink into his face from ear to ear. Blood gushes from between the Beast's teeth soaking Jed's camo jacket in two quick spurts. The Beast grinds it jaws, crushing Jed's facial bones to shards and pulp, while swallowing his dying screams like actual sustenance. Megan whimpers against her will and draws the attention of the Beast.

From deep within its primal mind the Urge begs, *scare her, hurt her before you kill her. For us.*

The Beast snarls and tugs and grinds. It clenches its jaws and gives a hard violent shake tearing away shredded flesh, ground bones, and strands of destroyed muscle from Jed's face. It stands to its full height in the moonlight, arching back with its glowing red eyes focused on Megan's trembling form. The moon almost reflects off the hard skin of the Beast while its fur negates the lunar glow completely. Its hard slender muscles twitch and it spits its mouthful of meat at Megan. She curses and tries to dodge the pulp that was seconds ago Jed's face but the Beast's aim is impressive. The gore splashes across Megan's face and chest with enough humiliating force it knocks her backwards, back into the mud, only semi-conscious.

Instinct drives her sloppily to her feet just in time for the Beast to pounce head-first at her. Its giant skull shatters four of her ribs (three on one side and one on the other) as it knocks her back down. Megan whimpers unable to take deep enough breaths to form a scream. The Beast stalks around her, sometimes on its hind feet and sometimes on all four powerful limbs, while inhaling the potpourri of her fear, blood, and urine.

Pain, sweet pain! Fear, sweet fear! Yes!

The Beast howls again and reaches its clicking claws towards the wounded woman. They tear away her blood-splattered yellow tank top and sundress in long colorful ribbons. Her American flag bra and matching thong are snapped away with twitches of the Beast's elongated fingers leaving her completely naked rolling around in the mud. Megan groans as she kicks wildly at the Beast's muscular legs and engorged genitals. It growls approval of her fight then reaches its claws down again; this time peeling away ribbons of her flesh from her arms, back, and sides as she rolls in frenzied agony.

Now, I feast!

The Beast leans down and does its best to curl the canine snout into a hellish smile. Suddenly it feels the cold steel barrel of the Mossberg stab into the crater of its right ear. The voices within don't even have time to speak before brains and skull bits splatter the tree next to the Beast. The monster-wolf sways on its hind legs, missing the entire left side of its massive head, before it tips over next to a crying Megan.

At sunrise, Declan stumbles naked and filthy from the tree line. His body feels both ravaged and refreshed. His shoulder bears scars from the mutilation the night before yet they look healed and aged with years rather than the ugly of morning after. His belly feels physically full yet hunger claws at his very soul. Declan climbs into the blood streaked cab and into the sleeping quarters to look for clothes. He rifles through Leon's stuff until he finds a faded Faith No More tee shirt, a less than hideous flannel, and a pair of jeans not completely oil stained. As he dresses he remembers the day and night before in quick flashes.

The truck driver they were going to rob turning into a goddamn werewolf.

The car crashing into the tree as he grabbed the wheel to stabilize the out-of-control semi.

The werewolf trucker attacking him but leaving him for dead to chase the others.

Sneaking up on them in the forest as the giant werewolf tortured Megan.

Stepping over a faceless Jed; his fists still clenching and un-clenching weakly.

Stabbing the tip of the Mossberg into the crater on the side of the werewolf's head and blowing its brains out the other side.

Declan drops into the driver's seat and spots his Aviators sunglasses on the floor. He picks them up and smiles at the sight of his blood streaked across the reflective lens. He licks them clean and dries them with a flap of his new flannel. The memories continue.

The pained relief in Megan's eyes when she saw him standing, smoking shotgun in hand, behind the fallen monster.

The terrible mewling sound she made when she realized he had used the last shred of his humanity to drop the wolf.

Falling on her, new fangs bared, and tasting her blood and meat. Feasting on Megan.

Feasting on faceless Jed.

Then, feasting on the middle aged couple trapped and hopeless in the smoking mess of metal across the street from the rest area.

Tonight is another full moon and Declan can feel it in his blood. He picks up Leon's yellow trucker's cap and puts it on. He doesn't even need to adjust it, it fits perfect. He smiles into the sunrise as he turns the key. With a rumble and a puff of black smoke the engine roars to life. Declan rolls down his window and flicks the volume on the radio. A shake and a hiss later the Full Moon Express is pulling back out onto the road.

FOUR WHEELS ON THE OPEN SEA

BY: MATTHEW VAUGHN

Agnes had spent the majority of her life in a wheel chair. A freak childhood accident had left her paralyzed from the waist down; she had no feeling at all, with the exception of her vagina. Down there she could feel everything, which worked out good for her when she ran away from home as a teenager and began living on the streets.

Life on the streets was tough, especially for a young girl in a wheel chair. But, like a lot of run-aways, she turned to a life of prostitution. It turns out there were a lot of men with fetishes that a girl like Agnes was suited for. Wheel chair fetishes, paraplegic fetishes, and she was a big hit with the anal crowd, seeing as she had no feeling back there she could take a pounding all night long.

As she got older, Agnes decided to leave the prostitution life after discovering porn paid a lot better. She had a good run as a porn star, and it was on set where she met the man who would become her husband, Woody, a camera operator.

The two quickly married, but because of work and money, never really got to take their dream honeymoon. They talked for years about taking a sea cruise aboard one of those big, luxury ships.

After retiring and pinching their pennies, they were finally able to fulfill their dream, with Agnes being sixty-six and Woody sixty-nine.

They chose an exciting sounding cruise ship interestingly named The U.S.S. Exciter. It was a senior's cruise, which would be perfect for them. No bothersome young people, everything on board tailored to people their age. Not to mention, it was fairly cheap as far as cruises go.

Agnes and Woody spent the majority of their time aboard the ship in their cabin. Woody had brought a fresh bottle of Viagra, so they spent many hours enjoying each other.

When they weren't holed up in their cabin doing the nasty, they did some exploring of the ship, and discovered that it wasn't very accommodating to wheel chair bound passengers.

There were a surprising amount of stairs and steps on the ship. There were whole levels Agnes was cut off from, unless Woody carried her up or down the stairs. Some steps just seemed randomly put on floors. Another annoyance was a high lip in every door way. Was it there to make the rooms sealed tighter? Maybe if the ship took on water? Agnes didn't know, but she could definitely do without.

Despite these issues, after an evening of passion with Woody, Agnes decided to take a roll around the ship, alone. Woody had already fallen asleep, his massive Viagra erection making a tent with the blankets, but Agnes didn't feel quite ready to sleep yet. The floor their room was on happened to be the same level as the deck. Agnes had no issues, other than the lips in the door ways, rolling out into the cool night. She could see lights on in some of the cabins, but she was all alone out on the deck. It was quite peaceful.

"Good evening my dear," a voice said from behind her. It startled her; she hadn't heard anyone walk up. She turned to see a well dressed, younger man. His clothing looked much too old for a person his age.

"Uh, hi. I thought I was alone out here," she said. She felt a little uneasy; this man didn't really belong on this ship.

"Allow me to introduce myself, my name is Horace…" he stopped mid-sentence, his eyes getting wide.

Horace started walking towards Agnes, so she began to roll backwards. She didn't go far, she backed into the railing. He came up beside her, and crouched down next to her wheel chair.

"The way the moon light shines off your chair, it's so wonderful," he said. He rubbed his hand around the chrome of the wheel and along the frame work.

"Uh, thank you?" she said, feeling very uncomfortable. Horace looked up at her like he was seeing her for the first time. He stood up and straightened his waist coat.

"Oh, uh, what was I saying? Yes, my name is Horace Dracul, and you my dear, shall become my next meal!"

Agnes was caught in his stare, compelled to sit right there as if she wasn't in any danger. Horace came for her, teeth bared, ready to dig in, when he heard something from over past the railing. He left Agnes sitting and went over to look. He could see out across the ocean, the moon illuminating the top of the water. He looked out and saw splashing in the water and imagined a large sea creature, with suction cup covered tentacles breaking the surface.

There was a squeak behind him and he was pulled from his thoughts. Horace turned away from the open sea and saw Agnes quickly rolling away from him. He cursed himself under his breath and took off after her.

Agnes was turning her wheels faster than she ever had before. Her hands were burning as she pushed herself to go faster and faster. She didn't understand why she had been sitting there so calmly while he came to kill her, or eat her, or whatever his plan was. But the moment she realized she could move again she did just that.

She wasn't too far from getting off the deck and back into the hallway with the cabins. She thought if she could just get to her room she could wake Woody and he could take care of this creep.

The doors leading in opened automatically, which was definitely a plus in this situation. Agnes didn't slow down as she came to the door way, and she didn't prepare herself for the lip at the bottom. She hit it so hard it scooted her forward in her chair. She was lucky that she wasn't thrown out of her seat.

Adjusting herself, Agnes went to lean her chair back when she started rolling backwards. She turned to see Horace's smiling face as he rolled her away from the cabins.

"Not so fast my dear, we haven't even started yet," Horace said to her. Agnes began to scream.

***

Woody opened his eyes, something had woke him up. He laid there for a minute, his mind cloudy from having been asleep. There was a knock at the door, which must have been what woke him.

He got out of bed and pulled on a pair of flannel pajama pants. He was still sporting a large, Viagra erection that pushed back against his P.J. bottoms. As he walked to the door of the cabin he glanced in the bed and noticed Agnes wasn't there. He didn't think that was too strange, she was known for not being able to go straight to sleep after a session of sex.

Looking out the peephole on his cabin door, Woody saw an empty hallway.

"What the crap?" he said. He turned to walk away when there was knocking again.

This time, Woody didn't bother looking through the peephole. He grabbed the door handle and threw the door open quickly. Agnes sat there in front of him.

"Oh, hey. Did you forget your key or something?" Woody asked her.

"Yes, I did," she replied. Woody looked at her for a moment.

"You sound funny, I hope you're not getting sick from being on this cruise," Woody said. Finally, he turned and walked away. When he made it back to the bed he watched Agnes as she pushed herself over the lip on the door way with ease, and rolled into the room.

Woody lay back down on the bed, his boner pitching a tent in his pants. He watched Agnes roll up to the foot of the bed. She peeled her shirt off and her sagging, wrinkled breasts bounced. She reached out and laid her hands on the bed, then lifted herself out of the wheel chair and onto the bed.

"Well, you seem oddly strong," Woody said.

Agnes just smiled and crawled across the bed, her arms holding her upper body weight, her lower half was dragging behind her. She pulled herself across Woody, making sure her breasts hit his erect dick on the way by.

"You ready for another round are ya?" Woody said.

She pulled herself onto his chest, her face above his. He looked down at her sagging tits, he loved those tits, even if they didn't sit up on her chest the way they used to. Woody smiled. Looking at Agnes's tits always put a smile on his face. He looked back up to her face and lost his smile. Agnes had her teeth displayed, fangs and all. She had the look of a very hungry animal.

"What the hell?" he said.

Agnes growled and went towards Woody's face, but he threw her off of him.

"Agnes, what's gotten into you?" Woody said. He stood up at the side of the bed. Agnes was still on the bed, her upper body being propped up by her arms.

"I've met someone else honey, he changed me in ways you will never understand," Agnes said. She bared her fangs again.

Woody backed around the bed until he got to the foot by where her wheel chair. Agnes turned in the bed, following his movement.

"Look, babe, I don't know what's going on, but we can get through this together," Woody said.

Agnes didn't respond with words, instead, she lunged at him. Woody turned and ran for the door. Agnes leaped off the bed and crawled across the floor behind him. When Woody reached the door he turned to see Agnes coming up quick. He couldn't believe how fast she could crawl. He was frozen with terror as she raced up to him. He knew he needed to turn around and open the door but he couldn't will his body to do it. Just then her expression changed. She stopped crawling and looked behind her. Woody looked too. The tubes running to her colostomy bag had pulled tight, stopping her from moving forward anymore.

Agnes looked from her bag attached to the wheel chair to Woody standing there staring at her. She growled at him and he snapped out of his trance finally. He whirled around and yanked the door open. Woody didn't spare a look back as he took off running.

Agnes crawled to her chair and threw herself into it. She quickly exited the room, and being able to roll the wheel chair so fast, Woody didn't really have much of a lead on her. He knew it too; he could hear her coming up behind him fast. He pumped his legs, but he was pushing seventy so they didn't move like they used to. Plus, his massive erection flopping back and forth was extremely uncomfortable.

The best idea Woody could come up with was to duck into a room and either find help or a weapon. The first couple of doors he tried were locked. But, then his luck hit when he tried a knob and the door came right open. He jumped inside and slammed the door shut.

Woody worked for a lot of years in the porn industry; he saw a lot of weird stuff, a lot of crazy fetishes. But, he was still taken off guard by what was happening in that room.

The first thing he saw was an extremely old man, naked, with his hands tied to the top of a walker and his feet bound to the bottom legs. Behind him stood an equally old woman who was gray bush deep into the old man's asshole with a strap-on.

On the bed in front of those two, an elderly lady laid spread eagle while another naked old man had one hand up to his wrist in her ass and his other hand up to his wrist in her vagina.

Next to the couple, an old man was also on the bed, on all fours, a naked old lady shoving her face in between his ass cheeks.

There was so much gray hair, wrinkles, and sagging skin everywhere. An old person orgy, that's one thing Woody could cross off his list of things he hoped to never see before he died.

When Woody shut the door, all the naked old people stopped what they were doing and looked first at his face, then at his erection.

“Hey there sonny,” the old man tied to the walker said. “I think we could make room for that mighty rod you’re packin!”

Before Woody could respond, the door behind him shook on its hinges as something rammed it on the other side. That something was Agnes.

Woody took off across the room just as the door flew open. Agnes wheeled herself into the room and scanned its occupants. No one moved, all the elderly people involved in their orgy were confused as to what was happening.

Agnes smiled, and then she attacked. She rode into the room, growling. The old man tied to the walker whirled around and fell backwards, pinning the old lady with the strap-on. Agnes grabbed the woman whose face had previously been buried in an old man’s asshole. Agnes tore into her neck and blood covered the bed and everyone on it.

Woody had managed to get himself into a closet while the chaos ensued. The old man tied to the walker was still on the floor and still on top of his lover with the strap-on, both screaming. One may have broken a hip. The old man fisting the old lady still had both of his hands inside of her, and in his panic he couldn’t compose himself enough to straighten his hands out and remove them. They were both screaming, and she was bleeding profusely as she twisted and turned, wanting to get away but unable to. Agnes had made short work of the salad tossing old lady and started in on the old man.

Woody watched it all as he managed to piss himself out of his erect dick. Agnes tore through the entire room. She leapt from her chair onto the back of the senior citizen that still had his hands tearing up the orifices of his partner. Agnes' weight pulled the man down and his hands finally released from inside the other woman's cavities. The golden ager on the bed was torn open, her asshole and vagina had become one giant hole. She didn't move anymore.

Woody's stomach turned at all the viscera and sinew strewn about the room. There was Agnes, on the bed, rolling around in the blood and guts from her victims. He couldn't remember the last time he had seen her so happy. Then he thought back to their love making earlier in the night and he had to suppress the bile that forced its way into his throat.

"Agnes!" Woody yelled at her as he busted out of the closet. "What have you become? I love you Agnes. I always will, but you're acting like a monster!"

Agnes laid there in the bloody mess she had created, watching Woody and listening to his words. She could still feel her humanity inside of her.

"This isn't so bad that we can't fix it," Woody said. He waved his hands around and tried not to look at the bodies, or partial bodies. "We can get through this, me and you. We can continue our little vacation on this cruise. If we need to get you some help when we get back, that's no big deal."

She felt like maybe he was right, maybe they could continue on as they had been before she changed. She could control this, she wasn't a monster.

"I love you, baby, and I want to work… ugh!" Woody said as he slipped on some lower intestines that were strung across the floor. Woody fell back and smacked his head on the floor, busting it open.

Ignoring everything Woody had just said, Agnes threw herself off the bed and onto him. She tore into his leaking skull with an intense fervor.

***

Surprisingly, Agnes did manage to hold onto some of her humanity, after she finished feasting on Woody she felt remorseful. She climbed into her chair, scooped up what was left of Woody's body and wheeled it out onto the deck. She went to the railing and looked out into the open sea. It was still dark out, the moon the only light to see by. She slung Woody over her shoulder, grabbed the wheel chair with one hand, the railing with the other, and threw them both out into the water.

INVISIBLE AGENT: NOW YOU SEE ME

BY: SCOTT CLARINGBOLD

Kate Griffin heard the tell-tale creak of the floor-board at the top of the stairs, which announced the return of her husband.

Somewhere between awake and peaceful slumber she thanked her lucky stars that Mark had made it home safely again.

Three glasses of wine with dinner had made it impossible for Kate to stay up to greet Mark.

Sleep coaxed her back to her dream. She was aware of Mark pulling back the covers. She felt his hands gently caress her shoulders, tugging the straps of her night-dress down her arms.

Still with eyes closed, Kate quivered as Mark's breath blew against her neck, his lips planting soft kisses.

Fingers massaged her chest, gently pinching her nipples. Those same hands moved down her body, stroking the tops of her legs.

She began to writhe under his weight.

Kate opened her eyes, expecting to see her husband's face, but... nothing.

She flung an arm across her breasts, cursing under her breath. Kate lashed out with a fist, hoping to catch Mark in the shoulder, her knuckle connecting with something more solid. His chin, perhaps.

'How may times do I have to tell you that creeps me out?' Kate hissed.

Mark, lying next to her but still invisible, chuckled. 'Sorry, I saw you there and couldn't resist.'

'Be quiet. I don't want to have to explain to our daughter why I'm talking to thin air.'

The covers rustled, Mark apologized again and then she heard him leaving the bedroom.

Both of them struggled to sleep after that.

***

Mark Griffin sat at the breakfast table drinking a cup of coffee and reading the morning paper.

Kate entered the kitchen, fiddling with the clasp on one of her earrings.

'Can you pass the butter, please?' Mark asked his daughter. Fourteen year old Laura munched on toast, listening to her MP3 player. She either hadn't heard Mark or was feigning deafness.

'It's like I'm invisible around here,' Mark joked. Kate shot him a look that Mark felt could have frozen his heart right there.

'You're okay for picking Laura up after school, right?' Kate asked, slipping on her high heel shoes.

Mark nodded as he crunched on his toast. 'Yeah, we should be done way before then.'

'Don't let me down.' She jokingly scolded Mark. Kate leaned in and kissed her husband and daughter before leaving the house.

'Just you and me, kiddo.' Mark said to Laura. Receiving no reply he stood up and cleared away the breakfast dishes.

Ten minutes later Laura clambered into the car, still with headphones fixed over her ears. Mark raised his eyebrows and his daughter reluctantly removed them. He understood of course - after all he had been young once. The band Sonic Thrust were Laura's life, she knew everything about them, from favourite colours to hottest sexual positions - which Mark wasn't too impressed with. But his daughter was growing up so fast.

'How's Kevin?' Mark teased, glancing at Laura as she blushed a rosy pink. Several weeks earlier Mark had been waiting for Laura at the school gates when he saw her walking with a boy. He could see that his daughter was flirting with this kid. Mark's first thought was to pull this lad to one side and give him a piece of his mind, but he refrained and instead asked his daughter about him. Mark had to concede that Laura wasn't Daddy's little girl any more and was more likely to go to her mother for advice than ask her dad.

'I don't think he even knows I exist.' she shrugged. 'It's like I'm invisible to him'.

Mark nodded, 'Believe it or not I can relate to that, sweetheart. It's his loss.'

'You have to say that, you're my dad.'

"True, but it's a well known fact that dads can't lie to their daughters.'

Laura looked at the goofy grin plastered over Mark's face and she laughed.

'You're such a loon.'

***

With Laura dropped off Mark began the two hour journey to London. Other than shouting 'Dick-head' at a couple of motorists it was an uneventful trip. Once in the heart of the city he headed for one of the newer buildings, fighting for supremacy among the other equally unique structures.

The Obsidian was a tall office block, made from impossible angles and smoked, black glass.

This was home to Ravenmore Security.

Six months ago

Mikel Dragovitch could feel his heart hammering in his chest, nausea threatened to climb from his gut, up his throat. The adrenalin rush gave him tunnel vision, he was intent on one thing and one thing only.

Mikel had never felt so alive. Which was more than could be said for the dead couple he had shot minutes earlier. The young man had died instantly, a bullet shredding his brain from close range.

The woman had taken a few minutes to die. Mikel studied her as she lay gasping for breath, like a fish out of water. Her skin had turned very pale, big blue eyes wide with fear. Mikel stopped beside her and brushed her hair from her face. He stared into her eyes, taunting death to come and look for him.

He tuned out the cries of the other hostages in the banking hall, he was tempted to drop his pants and have this woman before her life ebbed away. He would be the last thing she would see and feel.

The sirens outside distracted him long enough for the woman to give her death rattle. The room was starting to stink of the fresh, rusty smell of blood. The crimson liquid pooling under the couple.

Mikel turned his attention to the other hostages, an elderly man lay next to a young girl of around ten years old - his grand-daughter, and a man in an expensive Italian suit - looking like he might shit himself at any minute. Mikel's eyes stopped on the woman in the gym clothes. From the look of her she hadn't seen much of the inside of a gym but Mikel wasn't too picky if the truth be told.

***

In the bank vault Tommy Ridley was struggling to breathe.

'Stop panicking.' Joe Carter said, patting his friend on the back.

'No one ...said anything about.. about murder.' Tommy whispered, between sharp breaths.

'I know. He's shagging our Gemma and I thought he would be extra muscle. Let's just fill these bags and get the hell out of here.'

Tommy nodded his understanding, he stepped over the prone body of the bank manager who had been knocked unconscious after the robbers had gained access to the vault.

As the pair clattered about, emptying the cages there was the faint sound of broken glass.

'You hear that?' Joey asked.

Tommy nodded. 'Yeah, you think it's the cops?'

'We got hostages, they wouldn't be that stupid surely.'

***

Two minutes later and Mikel was wondering what was keeping those two English idiots. He had already decided to kill Tommy once the job was done. Joey might be allowed to live seeing as he had shared his plan.

Mikel headed to the vault, his gun still trained on the people in the banking hall.

'Hey, what are you morons doing?' Mikel shouted in his thick Russian accent. There was no reply from Tommy or Joey.

Mikel shook his head contemplating his next move. He ducked into the vault to find his cohorts in a heap. Mikel's face crumpled into sheer confusion.

He made his way back out to the banking hall, a quick scan of the floor confirmed that all of the hostages were still where he had left them.

Mikel gripped the gun tighter in his hands. Had those two clowns knocked each other out?

From his left Mikel heard a sound. 'Pssst!'

Spinning round Mikel found... empty air. He lurched around to see if anyone had moved. Someone screamed. Mikel nearly laughed when he realised the cry had come from the businessman.

'Over here...' a voice from behind him and to the right whispered.

Mikel whirled around but was met by empty air again. There was a tap on his shoulder and then something walloped Mikel flush in the face. The big man fell down, unsure of what had happened. Mikel's hands clasped together, guided by some unseen force. Then his meaty fists began to hit him around his own head and face.

The hostages in the banking hall watched in confusion as their captor punched his own face in some twisted game of 'Stop hitting yourself.'

There was a sound from the front door and the hostages cried out as one. Two armed police men were kicking at the door, motioning for the people to come forward.

Seeing this, Mikel tried to rise to his feet but was met by an invisible boot to his gut. The villain fell to the floor, gasping for breath.

The hostages began to dash for the exit.

***

Ravenmore Security Headquarters.

Mark sat at the large round table and tried to concentrate on the presentation slides being shown on the screen.

All the other twenty two chairs were filled by a wide variety of people, scribbling notes on their tablet computers.

The reason Mark was struggling to concentrate was because of the woman standing in front of the table. Doctor Tilly Hardacre was dressed in her white lab coat, hair pulled back in to a tight pony-tail. Her small-rimmed glasses were perched precar-iously on her tiny button nose, hiding her bright blue-green eyes.

She wore almost no make-up that Mark could detect but her face gave off a lovely golden glow. However, he wasn't sure if that might have just been his imagination.

Mark loved his wife and until the moment he had met Tilly he would never have contemplated being with another woman. That had all changed a few months ago when he found that he couldn't stop thinking about Tilly.

He hadn't done anything about his feelings up to this point but he wondered how long he could hold back.

Gideon Ravenmore stepped forward as Tilly finished her presentation.

'Ladies and gentleman, the future of policing is here. It's our duty to secure the public safety by procuring this wonderful formula and I hope that Mr Griffin has been swayed by the results of our research.'

Heads swiveled towards Mark, all eyes fixed on him. He shifted in his chair and coughed, buying some time to get his reply together.

'Mr Ravenmore, I've thought long and hard about your proposal and it is with regret that I must decline your offer.'

There were gasps from some of the people around the table. Ravenmore scowled at Mark.

'You see,' Mark continued, 'this formula has been handed down through several generations of my family. I don't feel comfortable profiting from something that was entrusted to me by my father.'

'But we've just shown you comprehensive proof that with this formula we could drastically cut crime.' Gideon was trying to keep his voice calm, but his anger was rising to the top.

Mark put the palms of his hands on the table,

leaning forward he addressed the table. 'My friends, surely you can see the danger of what is being put forward. There is something Orwellian about the thought of invisible police. That is not something I want my name associated with.'

There were murmurs of agreement from the group. Ravenmore glowered at Mark.

'Will you consider taking some time to think about it, Mr Griffin?'

Mark shook his head. 'I'm sorry, my decision is final.'

This announcement seemed to signal the end of the meeting as everyone began to stand up, while some loped off looking for coffee - or perhaps something stronger.

Ravenmore bounded over to Mark. 'I'm not happy about this, Mr Griffin.'

'I really am sorry.' Mark said sincerely, holding out his hand in a friendly gesture. Ravenmore gave a nasty smile and shook Mark's hand. With a nod, Ravenmore took off.

Doctor Hardacre came over, her eyes seemed to sparkle in the light of the room. She gave a demure smile and touched Mark's arm. For a second he thought he could feel the sparks flowing through him. He had to stop himself from grabbing her and holding her close. Mark was troubled by these thoughts. He shouldn't be thinking this way, he was a happily married man.

'I admire a man who stands up for his beliefs.'

Tilly said.

'Thank you.' Mark replied, giving her his best smile.

'I was so looking forward to working more closely with you though.' Was it just Mark's imagination or was there something flirtatious about the way she said 'closely'?

'Perhaps there will be other projects that could use my expertise?'

'I hope I can find something.' Tilly said and sauntered off towards the door.

Mark's brain was shouting at him to avert his gaze but his eyes were having none of it.

***

In the safety of her office, Tilly took out a mobile phone from her desk. She quickly glanced around and then rang the solitary number in the contact screen.

The tone on the other end rang once and then was picked up. No one spoke.

'He declined. I'll have to go down another route.'

'Do it.' A gruff voice replied before terminating the call.

***

Mark looked at his watch. It was nearly 1 o'clock. He was going to have to get a hurry on if he was going to be in time to pick Laura up from school. With any luck he would get a clear run home. Mark took the stairs to the car park level under the building. It was just as fast as the elevators.

Reaching the car park Mark fumbled in his pockets for his car keys. Three vehicles down from his he saw Tilly putting her case in the boot of her car. The lab coat had gone, she wore a smart black suit and heels. Mark felt his heart flutter. He was going to have to walk past her to get to his car.

'See you again,' Mark shouted, trying to keep his eyes straight ahead.

'Yes, see you soon.' Tilly replied. 'I... er... I hope.'

There it was. The hook. She had him at her bidding. Mark turned and walked over to her. 'I'm married.' He blurted the words out but felt better for having got it off his chest.

'I know.' she said. Standing forward on her heels she stretched up on her tip toes and kissed him lightly on the cheek.

'I need to get back for my daughter.' Mark said. He desperately wanted to kiss Tilly back. His mind was exploding with all sorts of thoughts.

'I'm sorry.' Tilly said, backing away towards her car. 'I shouldn't have done that.'

'No,' Mark reached out to her, pulling her back to him he planted a rough kiss on her lips. 'I shouldn't have done that either.'

***

Twenty minutes later and Mark was stood at the reception desk of a nearby hotel. Tilly stood off to one side busily checking her mobile phone. The reception manager looked Mark up and down, a look of revulsion on his face.

'I'm sorry sir. We don't rent rooms by the hour.' the man sniffed.

'How much for one night?' Mark asked.

'Will you be staying the full night?' the manager asked with his eyebrows raised.

Mark huffed and took out a credit card. 'Bill me for one night. If we're out of here in a couple of hours you can let the room again. If not then you haven't lost anything.'

The man looked over at Tilly, wrinkled his nose but accepted the card from Mark. Five minutes later and the couple were heading to room 225.

Mark was now stood in the bathroom, his hands gripping the side of the wash basin as he looked at himself in the mirror. 'I shouldn't be doing this. What do I think I'm getting here that I don't get at home.'

He took a deep breath and headed for the bedroom, intent on telling Tilly it had been a mistake.

Tilly was laying on the bed in mint green underwear and her high heels. She had let her hair down and it rested on her shoulders. Mark was momentarily stunned.

'You're a bit over-dressed.' Tilly teased. Mark chewed his bottom lip. 'Oh, you've had a change of heart.' she said, sitting up she pulled the sheet across her half naked body.

Mark looked at her, stood up and began unbuttoning his shirt. Within moments he was down to his shorts.

Tilly had removed her bra. He ran his hands up her legs and went to remove her briefs. He felt a sharp sting in the back of his neck. Mark looked up to see Tilly sitting back, a needle in her right hand.

Mark clasped the back of his neck as the room spun. He didn't have time to ask any questions before he clattered to the floor.

Tilly clambered off the bed, kicked at Mark's prone body, and then made a call.

***

Kate took a bite from the sandwich. Egg, not her favorite. Add to that the fact the bread was starting to curl in the heat and it wasn't the best lunch she had ever had.

She threw the sandwich on the desk, slumping down in her chair. Several files were stacked on the side of her desk courtesy of her boss Douglas. He had walked away with the parting shot that he wanted the accounts finished that evening.

Needless to say Kate was pissed off. She glanced at the wall clock. Ten past three. Mark should have picked Laura up now. Kate decided she would give them twenty minutes to get home and then she would give them a quick call. She was going to have to apologize to Mark that she would be late home.

Kate took a sip of her coffee. She looked up to see Douglas walking down the other end of the room towards the door.

'No doubt going for a late liquid lunch, fat git.' She whispered to herself.

At that moment her favorite Bon Jovi song began to play in her desk drawer. Kate flung the drawer open and grabbed her phone. It was Laura.

'Hi sweetheart. Is everything ok?'

'No, dad's not here.' Laura said sulkily. 'I hate having to hang around. It makes me look sad and pathetic.'

Kate mentally cursed her husband, he had promised he would be there. 'I'm sure he has a good reason, honey. Have you tried calling him.'

"Duh! Course I have.' Laura snapped back sarcastically. 'Went to voicemail.'

'Look, I'll see if I can get hold of him.' Kate waited for her daughter to reply.

On the other end of the phone there was a muffled cry, followed by the slamming of a door.

'Laura? What's happening, baby?' The sound of footsteps grew louder as someone picked up the phone. 'Hello?' Kate said.

There was definitely breathing on the other end

before the connection was cut. Kate's mind reeled, she felt physically sick as panic rose in her.

She dialed Mark's number as she grabbed her bag and headed for the door.

***

Tilly jumped at the sharp knock on the door. She had spent the past couple of minutes trying to tug Mark's clothes back on. He lay on the floor, his shirt unbuttoned, missing his jacket and shoes. That would have to do.

'Who is it?'

'Room service.' a heavily accented male voice replied.

Tilly took a peek through the spyhole and flung the door open. The man behind the food cart was tall and slender, dressed in a black suit and tie. He looked Tilly up and down and the woman realised she should have dressed herself too.

The man pushed into the room without a word. He threw the linen cover on the cart back and scooped up Mark with little effort. When Mark was secreted in the bottom of the cart the man nodded at Tilly and left.

Tilly dressed quickly. She removed some anti-bacterial wipes from her bag and began to rub down any surfaces in the room that could harbor any fingerprints.

***

Kate pulled up outside the school. She was frantic as she had been trying to contact Mark and Laura but without any success. A call to the police had proved fruitless even when she had mentioned who her husband was.

'They have probably just gone shopping or something.' The unhelpful policeman said. 'We can't really do anything for twenty four hours.'

Well, Kate could do something and she would. The car screeched to a halt and she clambered out of the drivers door. It had taken her a good forty minutes to get to the school, which was now mostly in darkness.

Kate looked up and down the street. There were a few teenagers kicking a ball around and talking too loudly. They were heading away from the school, back towards the village.

A few hundred yards away, the engine of a silver van sputtered to life and began to move slowly towards her.

With the mobile phone still glued to her ear, Kate flagged the van down. Maybe the driver had seen something that would help her.

The window on the drivers side rolled down and a bald headed, stocky man glared at her.

'Sorry for stopping you. I'm wondering if you may have seen my daughter.' Kate flipped through her phone for a photo of Laura and held the screen up to the man.

The driver looked thoughtful and got out of the vehicle. 'I think I might have seen her.'

Kate wasn't an expert on accents but she was sure that the man was Eastern European. Possibly Russian. The man made his way to the side of the van.

He pulled open the side door and beckoned Kate to come closer. Without thinking, Kate sidled up to him.

Laura lay on the floor of the van. A nasty mark was forming under a swollen eye. The girl was unconscious. The man gripped Kate's neck with his meaty paw, 'Get in. Don't make a noise or I'll kill you both.'

Kate was reeling, her mind spilling over with all kinds of scenarios. Her legs buckled under her.

Within minutes she lay next to her daughter, a piece of duct-tape stuck over her mouth, hands and feet bound with plastic cable ties.

How could she have been so stupid.

***

A searing pain and a blinding white light behind his eyes woke Mark up. He was disorientated due to the darkness of the cramped space.

He realised he was in a car boot. A hand went to the back of his head and came away wet and sticky. His other hand patted at his body, his jacket was gone. Mark swore out loud. His only vial of the invisibility formula had been in his coat pocket.

It came to Mark that he had also been carrying his grandfather's diaries. If they and the formula had fallen into the hands of rogues then he really didn't want to think of the consequences.

Mark listened through the boot to see if he could discern any distinguishing noises, but all he could hear were the tires on the road and muffled music from the radio.

No one had spoken so Mark guessed that there was only one person in the car. Those were good odds. Unless others were waiting for him when the car stopped.

He was unsure how long he had been laid out for. That made it difficult to try and estimate any location. The lack of any other traffic sounds made him think that they might be on a back road out of towns and cities.

A slowly dawning realization began to fall into place as Mark thought of Tilly Hardacre. She had set him up. Hook, line and sinker.

Was she driving the car? Could he pry open the boot and make a run for it now? Tilly had been wearing heels when he last saw her. Would she be able to catch him if he made off? On the other hand it may be night time out there and Mark didn't have a jacket or shoes. How long would he last if it was freezing cold?

A mobile phone rang inside the car. It was

Mark's ringtone. Someone answered, too deep and husky to be a woman.

Mark fretted about who was on the other end.

***

It wasn't long before the car pulled off the road and on to a gravel driveway. Mark heard the unmistakable sound of small chippings bouncing off the bottom off the car.

The vehicle eventually came to a stop and Mark heard footsteps and mumbled chatter. He braced himself for the boot opening. If this was to be the last stand of Mark Griffin then he was going down swinging.

Someone outside knocked on the boot, a tinny, metallic tapping sound.

'Hello,' said a voice that Mark recognized but couldn't quite place. 'Before you come out all guns blazing I should warn you that we have your family with us.'

Mark's usually confident exterior crumbled. He felt his shoulders sag at this statement. They had Laura and Kate. Or did they? Perhaps it was all just a bluff to get him to co-operate. He knew that people would be in his house now, looking for the formula ingredients.

'I'm not stupid.' Mark bellowed. Trying to make his words sound as if they had conviction. 'I wouldn't have all the formula written down. There is one ingredient that is passed down by word of mouth.'

There was raucous laughter from outside. The boot popped up and someone shone a powerful torch straight in Mark's face. Hands grabbed him on either side and hauled him out of the car. Mark landed heavily on the loose stones. He was outside his own house.

A couple of boots laid in to him. Mark felt the wind escape his lungs, a rib cracked and intense pain flared up his right hand side.

'Enough.' A voice commanded. Mark finally knew who it was. Gideon Ravenmore. The bulky man squatted down next to the injured Mark. 'Don't be a hero or Laura and Kate might meet a sticky end.'

'I want to talk to them, now!'

'You're not in control here, Griffin. Besides, your girls are a little... tied up at the moment.'

Mark made to jump up but the pain kept him where he was. A car door opened and Tilly Hardacre stepped out, like some socialite heiress posing for paparazzi. She had pulled her hair back into the ponytail and she wore a powder blue suit. The woman strode over to Gideon and planted a kiss on his cheek.

'You really should be more careful about who you take to hotel rooms.' Gideon said, making a tutting sound.

Mark hoped that Kate and Laura were out of

ear-shot. It was only because Tilly had knocked him unconscious that he hadn't slept with her. He hadn't done the deed and deep down he thought he might not have gone through with it, but he knew he probably would have.

'Where are my family?' Mark growled, spitting the words with venom.

'The formula?' Gideon asked, eyebrows raised.

Tilly walked over to Mark. She tugged him by the arm and Mark stumbled to his feet. 'Just tell him. He always gets what he wants, make it easy on you and yours.'

Mark sneered at her. 'Is that what you did, make yourself easy? How much did he pay you to trap me?'

Tilly whistled, 'A lot. Probably enough for me to take off abroad, assume a new identity and never have to work again.'

Mark could feel hate well up inside him. He clenched and unclenched his fists. Digging his nails into the palm of his hands.

There was a sharp clap behind Tilly. The woman's mouth formed a tiny circle of shock and surprise. Mark saw the small red dot of blood on Tilly's chest. It quickly blossomed like a flower. Spilling bright red liquid onto the gravel.

Tilly tried to talk but all she could manage was the sound of sucking in air. She fell forward and Mark caught her.

Gideon Ravenmore lowered the gun. 'Always

was a gobby cow that one. As if I was going to pay her all that money.'

Tilly stared into Mark's eyes as she died. He thought she was trying to tell him she was sorry. He gently lay her on the path. 'I'm sorry too.' he whispered.'

'Touching.' Gideon said. 'Now quit the bullshit and tell me where the formula is.'

Mark slowly nodded his head. The feeling of helplessness had settled on his shoulders. If he didn't do what this madman wanted then his wife and daughter could be the next ones laying here.

'I'll take you.' Mark said. 'It's hidden in a secret compartment that you would never find. But first I want to see my family.'

Gideon seemed to contemplate this request. 'Take me to the formula and before you open it I will let you see your family.' He smiled, a sinister twist of his lips.

Mark began to walk to the house, a couple of thugs landed in next to him. The front door was already open. Mark was on familiar territory now. In a fight he would hold all the cards. He knew every nook and cranny of this place and he would use it all to his advantage.

Mark's heart sank when he saw Molly curled up in a corner. 'What did you bastards do to my dog?'

Mark received a sharp dig in his back from one of his captors. He led them to the kitchen as Ravenmore followed them. At a long wall Mark stopped and rounded on Ravenmore and his men.

'Ok, where are my family?' he asked, his voice quiet.

Ravenmore took a mobile phone out of his pocket. 'Bring them in. So, how does this work?' Gideon asked, turning to Mark and indicating the wall.

Mark didn't reply, standing his ground. He wouldn't move another muscle until he had seen his family.

Moments later three figures entered the kitchen. Mark's breath caught in his throat when he realized who was with his wife and daughter. But this was quickly replaced with anger when he saw Laura's swollen cheek and eye.

He pushed forward ready to tear Dragovich's head off but was stopped by one of the other men.

'Nice to see you.' Dragovich drawled, stroking Kate's face. 'Me and Mrs Griffin have been getting to know each other.' He gave a cheeky wink and smiled at Mark.

Ravenmore tutted. He had had enough of all this. 'Right, give me the sodding formula, now!'

Mark looked at his wife and held out a hand. 'I need the key to open it.' Kate gave him a confused look. 'The key on your locket.'

She nodded her understanding and went to pull the locket from around her neck. The pendant was under her blouse. A hand clamped around hers. Dragovich tore at Kate's blouse, exposing her chest.

He yanked the chain and the links twisted and split as it came away.

Mark was furious, he stormed forward and punched Dragovich in the face. Bringing his hand away, Mark was fairly sure that that had hurt himself more than Dragovich.

Ravenmore pushed his gun in to the side of Mark's head. 'Such a display of affection for someone you were cheating on only hours ago.'

Mark's heart sank. He watched as the words seeped into Kate's brain. Her face twisted into a mask of horror.

'What's he talking about.' Kate asked.

'Nothing happened.' Mark said. His mind visualized Tilly lying on the gravel outside, but the face was that of his wife.

'But it would have done. If Tilly hadn't knocked you out.' Ravenmore was enjoying this far too much Mark thought. 'Open it.'

Mark stepped towards the wall and located the sliding panel, he turned slightly to catch Kate's attention, she still had a look of confusion etched on her face. He would make it up to her somehow. Ravenmore had been right, if Tilly hadn't stopped him then Mark would have slept with her.

He pushed those thoughts aside. For now his priority was getting his family away from here, he nodded at Kate and blinked hard twice. Reaching in to the panel, Mark flipped a switch and the lights went out.

He grabbed the shotgun and threw it across the room. Kate had been waiting for it and it almost landed right in to her hands. She lifted the butt of the gun up and smashed it into Dragovich's face. It caught him flush in the nose, blood gushed down his chin as he sat down hard.

Kate grabbed Laura by the hand and they took off, running. 'Stay with me, baby.'

Mark was taking care of the other two thugs, he had retrieved a handgun from the panel and had dispatched one of the men as the lights went out.

Now he was locked in hand to hand combat with the other bruiser. His gun already lost in the melee. Fists and feet flew in fast as the two men sized each other up. But one thing that the thug hadn't counted on was that Mark had also picked up a vial of invisibility formula from the hiding place and he quickly swigged it down.

Within moments he began to disappear. His attacker was soon on the floor, doubled up in pain as unseen feet kicked him. Mark was wincing as the pain shot through his shoeless feet.

A bullet whizzed past very close to Mark's ear. Ravenmore aimed again. Mark dropped to the floor and clambered to where Ravenmore stood. He swept his leg round in an arc and the bulky man tumbled backwards.

Ravenmore laughed. 'Bravo, Mark. Always pays to have an exit strategy. Time I showed you mine.' He removed a small black device from his pocket.

Mark had scurried away to the other end of the room. He was crouched behind the kitchen table, wondering how to get out of here and what the hell that silly old sod was on about.

Ravenmore pressed the device and... nothing happened. Mark nearly chuckled until he saw Dragovich on the floor, hands clasped to the side of his head, howling in agony.

An astonishing transformation took place. Hair began to rapidly sprout all over Dragovich's body, his muscles bulged as bones twisted into new shapes. His face became contorted, pushing outwards and forming a snout. His teeth grew razor sharp in his large mouth.

The whole scene took mere seconds but felt like a lifetime, as if it was happening in slow motion.

Mark realized that Ravenmore had been searching for more than just the invisibility formula.

Ravenmore stood before Dragovich, arms out and smiling as if he was welcoming home the prodigal son.

'So many secret formulas out there, Mark. Some nearly as old as yours.' Ravenmore's voice was controlled, measured. He was utterly confident that Mark was still in the room. 'Do yourself, and your family, a favor and just hand over the invisibility formula and we'll be on our way.'

Mark doubted the sincerity of Ravenmore's words. Especially after what had happened to Tilly.

Mark decided to make a break for it.

***

Kate and Laura were running, a whirlwind of emotions cascading through their heads. Within a minute they were passing the body of Tilly, spread on the gravel, blood starting to dry.

Laura nearly let out a scream when she encountered the body, but Kate gently turned her daughter's head and looked deep into her eyes.

'Don't think about it. Follow me, stay as quiet as you can.'

Laura nodded, Kate glanced back. There had been the sounds of a scuffle. She hoped her husband was alright. There were no shouts or footsteps following them so that was a good sign.

When they had moved to the village Mark had been insistent that they install a panic room under the garage. With a combination that only he and Kate knew. In his role of Freelance Consultant to the Metropolitan Police he wanted to be sure that criminals would not be able to exact any retribution on his family.

Kate silently thanked his stubbornness, she had honestly thought that they would never need such a facility.

It was then that they heard the blood-curdling howl coming from the kitchen.

***

Mark was on his feet and running, with a look behind him he could see the Wolf-thing that had been Dragovich, sniffing the air. Despite the animalistic appearance the gleaming yellow eyes showed signs of malevolent intelligence.

Mark's thoughts turned to his family. Strange how your mind works when your under pressure. Drago-wolf could catch up with him any second and rip him limb from limb but his thoughts were not for his own safety but that of his girls. He grew angry at the thought of anything happening to Laura.

Ravenmore was laughing, a demented cackle that reminded Mark of a nut job villain from that superhero cartoon he couldn't remember the name of.

'All you had to do was give me the formula, Mark. It would have saved you and yours a messy end.' Ravenmore shouted. 'He's all yours.'

With that Drago-wolf smashed through the back door, knocking it clean off its hinges.

The invisibility formula chose that moment to wear off. 'Shit.' Mark fled away from the house hoping to lure the wolfman with him. But Drago-wolf had stopped, a wicked smile curled his black and twisted lips. The beast turned and hurried towards the garage.

'Oi, dick-head.' Mark jumped up and down, waving his arms. He knew it was pointless. Dragovich had smelled Kate and Laura and was going for them instead. Mark turned on his heels and began to run towards Dragovich.

There was a sound, a thunderclap that reverberated around the area. Ravenmore stood at the back door

***

Inside the garage, Kate was on her knees behind the old camper van that Mark had attempted to fix up. In front of her was a small hatch that resembled a simple drain cover except for the sophisticated time lock that was counting down. Mark had had this fitted nearly fifteen years ago, he had only told Laura the combination once. Every time someone put the wrong number in the device would lock them out and add another minute to the countdown. Kate was on her third attempt.

Why couldn't she remember it? Anniversary, birthdays, none of them rang a bell with her as being the four digit number Mark had given her .

She looked up at Laura. The young girl smiled back. The bruise around her eye was darkening now but she would be alright. Laura was a fighter.

There was a noise from the front of the garage and then a beastly hand grasped Laura and dragged her backwards. Laura squealed with shock.

Kate gasped and grabbed for the shotgun that she had placed beside her. As she stood up, hauling the heavy weapon to shoulder height, she saw the gruesome face of Drago-wolf. She could still see his lecherous eyes staring from the creature.

A long, slimy tongue flicked out of the side of Dragovich's deformed mouth and licked Laura's face. Kate was thankful that her daughter had appeared to have passed out.

'Let go of my daughter you fucking creepy bastard.' Kate whispered, but still with an air of menace.

Drago-wolf began to wheeze and for a moment Kate wondered if perhaps it was a death-rattle and if the thing was in the throes of dying.

She was livid when she realized it was a taunting laugh. Goading her. Kate shrugged and her trigger finger happily obliged, spreading several fragments of werewolf skull over the ceiling, wall and floor.

The thing didn't even have time to react, its body twitched for several seconds before landing in a heap.

Kate kicked at the corpse but it was well and truly dead.

***

On leaving the garage Kate found Ravenmore's body on the back step, his neck twisted at such an impossible angle that forensic scientists would argue for decades to come if a man could have summoned enough force to do it.

The popular theory was that Drago-wolf had

murdered his employer. In the days that followed Ravenmore Security would move to distance itself from Gideon, saying he was a megalomaniac, obsessed with building an army of supernatural beings.

There was also no sign of her husband. Long after the police had drank all her coffee and eaten all the biscuits, Kate stomped around the garden with a stick, jabbing at pieces of earth.

Laura was worried that her mother had gone mad.

One day, while out in the garden, Kate felt a light breeze ruffle her hair and something touch the side of her face. For a moment she was reminded of her husband creeping into bed, while still invisible.

'Mark?' she whispered... but no-one answered.

FLOWERS FOR OPHELIA

By: Michelle Garza and Melissa Lason

They peered through the wrought iron bars of the fence, watching the fog gather about the sepulchers and crooked tombstones. The grand mortuary house sat at the center of the ancient cemetery, surrounded by high hedges that created a withered wall of thorns.

"Her casket's more like a treasure chest," Harper said. "Never have I seen anything like it."

"What about the mortician?" Andrews asked.

"Lives alone and sleeps like the dead," Harper answered, giggling at his pun. "Groundskeeper told me so."

"How're we gettin' in?" Andrews tugged at a heavy lock secured through a thick chain on the gate.

"Got us a key from Anthony, the grounds man,

he'll be waitin' to let us into the parlor."

"Let me guess, he's chargin' a big cut."

"An arm and a leg, he said," Harper answered, then burst into laughter. "Met him at the pub, he's a good man."

"Lay off the liquor!" Andrews said.

"All jokin' aside. He wants nothin' but the necklace around her neck…we take the rest."

"It's a deal."

"Damn right."

The chains rattling across the silent burial grounds made them wince as time seemed to slow with the fear of being found out.

"Hurry it up," Andrews urged.

"Calm down now, almost got it," Harper answered as the rusted old lock popped open.

The mist climbed up their legs, chilling their skin through their trousers. It was deep and thick enough to shroud them as they slipped between the tombs. Andrews kept his hand on the shoulder of his partner as they snaked through the cemetery, the distance between them and the funeral parlor seemed to stretch on forever. As they drew near the mortuary, Andrews sighed. He couldn't imagine getting lost among the ancient mausoleums and headstones. A cold radiated from the earth, penetrating the soles of their leather shoes. Andrews wanted nothing more than to have the job done.

"I heard something," Harper whispered, all the mirth had gone from his voice.

"Let's be done with this," Andrews answered nervously.

"Not until we get our reward," Harper said.

He eyed Andrews then nodded to the graves around them. "Nothin' down there but some dry old bones. Stop being yellow."

"This better be worth it," Andrews spat.

"I came to the viewin' this mornin'. If we leave with only a handful of her burial riches, we will be wealthy men."

They ran for the stone driveway that lead between the hedges and into the manicured yard of the mortuary.

"This way," Harper whispered, pointing to a side entrance. "He said he'd be waiting there."

The lawn was free and clear, not a wisp of fog clung to the earth there. Andrews wondered if it wasn't from the heat of the furnace the house more than likely employed to cremate corpses when requested. It did feel warmer once they left the hallowed ground of the graveyard behind, his apprehension abated slightly.

"There," Harper said and trotted for a door.

"Who goes?" A deep voice hailed them.

"Flowers for Ophelia," Harper answered.

A hulking shadow loomed there, utterly black beneath the clouded sky, only the red illumination of a lit pipe distinguished that he was there at all. As they drew closer Andrews could make out the features of the grounds man's face by the fire of his pipe, it was a gaunt visage with hollow cheeks and dark eyes. The man smiled, yet it only added to his ghoulish appearance.

"Evenin', gents." He spoke clear and loud.

Harper jumped at the volume of Anthony's voice.

"Don't you worry. He can't hear a thing."

"Are you certain?"

"Positive," The giant man answered. "Come now, it must be done before dawn."

Anthony opened the door and they followed him inside. The funeral parlor was over a hundred years old and only lit by lamps and candelabras. It smelled of freshly snuffed candles, only a few flickered here and there. Anthony took one up then beckoned the thieves to follow. He hurried them past the chapel area, its door was closed yet the window beside it was made of elaborate stained glass. They entered a hallway so narrow that the groundskeeper could barely fit between its walls.

Andrews did not like the feeling of being the last man in line, it felt as if the eyes of a hundred spirits were steadily piercing his spine. The hair on his arms and the back of his neck stood out, a jingle of keys caused his heart to stutter. He jumped, bumping into his partner who then fell forward into the hulk before them. Anthony spun, caught Harper by the neck with his free hand and held him there, just staring intensely into the thief's eyes.

"Remember what you promised me." He spoke

at last and released Harper who only nodded, rubbing his throat.

The groundskeeper turned back to open the door at the end of the hall. They rushed inside as Anthony shut it behind them. He used the candle he carried to light others about the small room that smelled of withering flowers, baby's breath and carnations. Thin white lines striped the floor as the moon appeared through the clouds in the sky beyond the shuttered windows.

The casket was ghost white, sitting in the center of the room on small stone pillars.

"There you are, old girl," Harper said smiling. "Come on, let's get what we came for."

Andrews was surprised when he viewed the corpse beneath the candle light. She was very young, far too young to have died. His eyes inspected her for any signs of a tragedy, a broken neck or any trademarks of terrible sickness, but found nothing since only her head was not covered with treasures. Harper hadn't lied when he spoke of riches, her casket was filled with small gold coins, rings set with sparkling jewels and about her neck was draped a silver chain adorned with a locket in the shape of a crucifix. Inside of it shown crimson. He held his breath wondering if it was ruby. His hands trembled, his apprehension left him as he ran his fingers through the bounty within her coffin. He no longer feared the graveyard with its fog shrouded tombs outside.

"Who was she?" Andrews asked.

"Says right here," Harper answered, running his hand over an engraving inside of the coffin lid. It was in a foreign language, yet he could make out a name. "Ophelia Alucard."

"She was beautiful," Andrews said staring down at her pale skin and coal black tresses.

"Indeed," Harper said as he pulled burlap sacks free that had been hanging from his belt. "Perhaps once we relieve her of some of them bobbles, there'll be enough room for you to hop in there with her and give'er a good knobbin'!" Harper laughed heartily.

Andrews shook his head.

"Get to gettin'," Harper said as he tossed a sack to his partner then started shoving handfuls of coins into his own bag.

The sacks grew heavy and clanked loudly as they deposited them beside the door. As they worked Anthony sat watch, once in a while peeking out the door or through the shuttered windows lining the viewing room.

"I'm not sure we can carry it all." Andrews laughed.

"We're sure as hell gonna try!" Harper answered.

They filled the bags until there were no more sacks to fill. Ophelia was still bathed in gold and silver, yet the men had nothing more to carry it out in. Her body was slowly revealed and Andrews stared down at her chest, beneath an elaborate burial gown was a con-caved area in her left breast.

Their celebratory giddiness came to a halt when they could hear the snort of a horse followed by hoof beats and the clattering of a carriage on the stone driveway.

"My necklace?" Anthony shouted. "Quickly!!"

Harper stuck his hand into the coffin, gripped the treasure and yanked it free from Ophelia. He held it out in the candlelight, it glimmered white like moonlight. Anthony held out a velvet sack and Harper slid it inside.

"Who's out there?" Andrews asked, grabbing sacks and preparing to run.

"Stay here," Anthony instructed and blew out his candle.

Harper went frantically about, snuffing out the rest of the candles then gripped Andrews by the shoulder.

"Do you think the constable was alerted? Perhaps the mortician awoke and went to fetch him?"

"We're in for it. Grave robbing is a serious offense," Andrews said.

He grabbed a sack, untied it then ran for the coffin.

"What the blazes are you doin'?" Harper asked.

"Let's put it back and run for it," Andrews answered.

"Nonsense. Let Anthony handle it," Harper said.

They listened closely, but could only make out

one voice speaking to the groundskeeper in English that came from a foreign tongue, a single sentence was clear.

"Flowers…for Ophelia."

They looked to each other in the darkness, anxiety built as they suspected betrayal.

Voices in the hallway sent them running for cover in the small room. They ducked beneath a visitor's pew as the commotion drew near.

Anthony flung the door open and behind him entered a figure cloaked in a black cape, in his hand he carried a bouquet of flowers. "The crucifix?"

It was not the constable at all. Harper, held his hand over his mouth, listening carefully over his own breathing and panicked heart to the conversation between the two men at the door.

"It was removed, master," Anthony said.

"The mortician?"

"I pulled his head from his shoulders."

"Very good," The stranger complimented.

Andrews nearly lost control of himself, his partner was promised that the funeral director slept like the dead…indeed the old man did because he was no longer among the living.

"You two, come out now. I can hear your hearts beating." The man spoke.

The thieves didn't move from their cover.

"I know you are here. Don't be fools."

He walked towards the casket and placed the bouquet upon Ophelia's chest.

"You may awaken now, my dear. The spell has been broken."

The stranger stepped back as a white hand gripped the side of the coffin. Ophelia came crawling from her bed of silver and gold, baring fangs like a serpent. Her eyes shined brightly like a predator beneath a hunter's moon.

"She is weak. She must feed to replenish her body."

Anthony went through the pews, kicking them over one at a time.

"Sorry, mates. I spent too long diggin' graves. He offered me a treasure much more valuable than gold, life unending for my servitude. Neither of us can touch the necklace, only a human could remove it, that's why I solicited you."

Harper scurried out as the groundskeeper reached their hiding spot. Anthony grabbed him by the back of his shirt and hauled him to his feet.

"Come out and maybe Mr. Dracula will make it quick." He said to Andrews who laid his face against the cold stone floor in defeat.

"My bride. I have searched for you so long. My foe thought he could hide you here, in this secluded cemetery…but he failed. Now that Van Helsing's amulet has been removed we can spend forever together." Dracula sighed, embracing the radiant creature known as Ophelia.

Harper broke free of Anthony's grip and ran for the door. Ophelia crossed the room in a single leap, falling onto the grave robber's back. She sank her teeth into his neck as he screamed. Andrews lifted his face to see his partner being drained of all of his life giving blood. His face was filled with terror and regret just before he fell dead from her grip. Andrews was lifted up to his feet by the strength of a single hand, Dracula dangled him there above the floor. He watched the wound in Ophelia's chest closing as she rose from Harper's corpse, her face covered with blood from her ravenous feeding.

"Anthony, gather the rest of the treasure and put it in the carriage. We shall join you shortly," Dracula instructed his ghoul.

Andrews trembled, a tear ran down his cheek as he began to pray. Dracula presented the human to his bride and nodded, then whispered to Andrews as fangs met his throat. "I don't think he's listening."

A six-foot hole had already been opened by the groundskeeper. It was meant for a white casket containing the corpse of a ravishing young woman. It was fed a coffin, only it held the bodies of two bloodless grave robbers. They were quickly buried beneath the headstone carved with the name Alucard and a bouquet was placed upon the earthen blanket covering them.

The black carriage parked just beyond the cemetery gate, heavy with gold and silver. Anthony slammed the rusty lock shut and climbed in the driver's seat, whipping the horses into a frenzied race against the sunrise.

THE CREATURE

BY: ESSEL PRATT

Concrete walls, bathed in prison gray latex paint, dribble an aura of depression and despair within the windowless room. High above, hanging like a noose from the ceiling, a single light bulb sways back and forth as cool air from the only vent blows gently into the room. Just below the bulb, a faded red fire sprinkler drips to the concrete floor below, puddled next to the three inch drain pipe that ascends below in the center of the room. The thick steel door had no viewing hole, nor were there any marks of a handle within. It was flush with the wall, not even allowing a breeze an invitation through. If any space within the world represented depression and despair, it was the room.

In the corner opposite the door, a creature, tall as a six foot man, shakes with anxiety upon the floor, its legs pulled tightly against his torso, his long arms wrapped tightly around just below the knees. His thick green skin, like that of an alligator, shivers uncontrollably, the webbing between his fingers and toes seize like the angry waves during an ocean storm. His blackened eyes blink to moisten the dryness and his chapped lips flake with each movement. He is frightened, anxious, pleading within his mind for reprieve from the torture.

Soft whimpers expel from his throat, deep hums vibrating his vocal cords to hoarseness, like an ancient hymn from the Lost City of Atlantis. The creature is mature in his age, yet not prehistoric enough to have lived in the days of old where the most advanced culture ruled the world. Although, beyond the walls, speculation meanders that he originates from sunken city, expelled from its walls, or lost while exploring the world beyond. Within the walls, he is alone and at the brink of demise as moisture evaporates from his flesh, leaving him parched and fatigued. If born of the Lost City, irony beckons as within the diminutive room he has lost his mind and lost his way.

Huddled in an upright fetal position, the creature's mind wanders as consciousness ebbs and flows from ire to morose dejection, to wretchedness to melancholy numbness. His body language reveals his loss of will to live. His sunken eyes show understanding of his damnation. His crackled leathery flesh crafts a tale of hardship within the craters and valleys that meander across his body, legends that are decided outside the walls as invisible eyes watch from afar.

As the creature huddles in solitude, the light above dims with a flicker and signals an oncoming flood of fear. Pipes in the ceiling flex as they expand as water races toward the sprinkler's sprayer. The creature stands upright with the speed of a frightened kitten, pushing his large body as close to the cold wall as he possibly can, anticipating the water's arrival into the room.

A moment of silence bellows within the room just before the swooshing sound erupts and sends scattered droplets all around, dousing the room in all directions. The creature, still shivering in fear, raises his arms to the air, spreading his fingers out wide, creating an umbrella with his webbing. Still, the water saturates his alligator skin, refreshing the leathery hide and revitalizing his parched vessel. Yet, the moisture is not welcomed by the creature, who's throaty murmur beckons for the flow to cease as he swats at the sprinkler, despite it being well out of his reach. His deep vibrato reaches a crescendo, expelling his fright into verbal substance, his quaking body climbing the Richter as tears flow from his blackened pupils. Panic emanates from within, his heart palpitates with the vigor of a furious pot of boiling water, and his every muscle tenses under the stress of uncontainable fear. The symphony of fear builds to a final climax and the creature collapses to the floor, out cold, exhausted at the distress he endured. The water flowing from the sprinklers stops and the single light bulb's brightness intensifies to its previous state. The labored breaths of the creature bounce off the walls within the room, accompanying the rhythmic flow of excess water down the lead pipe drain.

***

In another room, somewhere safely away from the creature, two men stare at a large monitor that is mounted to the soft white plastered wall. The brightly lit room radiates with monitors, gauges, and other flashing objects. The older man, treating the creature's collapse as a routine occurrence sips his steaming black coffee. He stares at the health monitors with interest as he types the results into a spreadsheet. The younger of the two, not more than a couple years out of college, watches the creature wide eyed with curiosity to rival the friskiest kitten.

"Is he okay?" asked the younger man. "Should we get him some help?"

"Don't bother," says the older man, slightly annoyed. "This happens multiple times each day. He's going to be fine."

"Was there something in the water?" asks the younger man. "He was pretty freaked out."

"Nope," the man takes a sip of his coffee. "He's just afraid of water."

“What? You mean to tell me that the creature, the very creature that was found in the lagoon is afraid of water?” The younger man isn’t buying it.

“Yes. That is exactly what I am saying,” the old-er man places his coffee cup on a napkin, dark rings absorb into the paper. “He wasn’t when we first met. But, he is now.”

The younger man takes his seat and grabs the carafe from the coffee pot. He is careful to fill his cup only half full before he returns it to the hot plate and grabs the shaker of powdered creamer, pouring enough in to fill the rest of the cup.

“How can that be?” he asks.

“The best we can figure, it is a form of post-traumatic stress disorder,” says the older man. “When we tried to capture him, he was swimming under the waves of the lagoon, stalking our small fishing boat. We knew his strength and prowess would surely result in him pulling us under. So, we tossed small grenades in the water, creating concus-sions that we hoped would knock him out cold. It took over an hour and a year’s salary worth of the grenades, but we did it.”

“Wow,” the younger boy sits on the edge of his seat. “Why not put him in an aquarium?”

The older man sits back in his chair, placing the palms if his hands on top of his head. “Too danger-ous, he’d get out. After the grenades, he is terrified of water. So, we stuck him in the cell, with a small camera in the corner to the right of the door to watch him, and sprinkle him a couple times a day so his skin doesn't dry out. At this point, we can only study him from afar. But, when he eventually dies, we'll take a more in depth look at what makes him tick."

"When do you think that will happen?" asks the younger man.

"No idea, so we wait."

Movement on the screen catches the younger man's attention and he turns his head toward it. The creature sits up, huddling in the corner with its legs pulled tight to its chest. His arms wrap tightly around, just under the knees, and a melodic hum emanates from his throat as he rocks back and forth.

"What now?" asks the younger man.

"We wait until his skin dries and do it again," says the older man, taking another sip of his coffee, the steam fogging up his glasses.

GASTROPODS OF TERROR

BY: SCOTT ERICKSON

The title bursts onscreen as orchestral music reaches a bombastic crescendo. After the final credit, the ridiculous music is replaced by the soothing chirping of crickets.

The camera pans to a parking lot which Menomonie teenagers refer to as “Lover’s Lane.” Actually, they refer to it as “Intercourse Alley” but let’s ignore those naughty teenagers and have some dignity. Perhaps if Menomonie had attractions more exciting than Bert’s Barbershop, local teenagers would have something to do other than trying to not accidentally get pregnant.

In the parking lot is a blue 1965 Mustang convertible. In the Mustang are Linda-Sue and Howie.

“Be gentle,” says Linda-Sue, “it’s my first time.”

“Really?” says Howie. “That’s not what I heard

at Bert's Barbershop."

"I mean, it's my first time in a 1965 Mustang convertible."

"Whatever," replies Howie. "Here, let me take off my pants."

"Oh my God!" shrieks Linda-Sue. "It's huge!"

"I'm glad you're pleased," offers a pant-less Howie.

"I wasn't talking about *that*," says Linda-Sue, pointing out the window, "I was talking about *THAT!*"

Suddenly, the silence is broken with really disgusting "slurping" sounds.

"Oh my God!" shouts Howie. "It's huge! But… what is it?"

"It's…It's…*OH MY GOD!!!"*

Suddenly the scene ends and we don't get to see what the hell made them scream in terror. What in God's name was it? A zombie? A psycho killer? A positive pregnancy test?

∞

In the CBS studios in New York, *The Late Night Talk Show with Johnny Kibble* is underway.

"Our next guest," announces Johnny Kibble, "is Peter Mollusk." Peter proudly walks on stage to the applause of the audience obeying the flashing "Applaud Like Crazy" sign.

After they're both seated, Johnny Kibble asks, "This is a joke, right? Your name can't really be *Mollusk.*"

"Thanks, Mr. Kibble. You can just call me Peter. I'm a *gastropodologist*. I'm the nation's leading expert on slugs."

"Slugs, eh? Okay, I'll play along."

"They evolved from snails. The same basic body design has independently evolved many times. In gastropodological terms, that means slugs are a surprisingly *polyphyletic* group."

A snickering Johnny Kibble says, "*Prophylactic?*"

The audience laughs.

"Well, since we've somehow broached the subject," says a smirking Johnny Kibble, "let's talk about the slug's *sex life!*"

"Sex life?"

"You know…what do mommy and daddy slug do to make baby slugs. In other words, Peter Mollusk, tell us how slugs make *the beast with two backs*."

"Strictly speaking, slugs don't have *backs*. They do, however, have *mantles*."

"Ladies and gentlemen, Peter Mollusk will now tell us about *the beast with two mantles*."

The drummer does a rim shot. The audience laughs.

"Okay, ladies and gentlemen," announces Johnny Kibble. "We'd like to give the opportunity to members of our studio audience to ask Peter anything about slugs. Yes—the elderly woman wearing gardening gloves and holding seed packets."

"I have a question about my garden," says the woman who stands to reveal she is also carrying a watering can. "I want to get rid of the slugs, but without using poison."

Peter answers, "Have you tried beer?"

"Mr. Mollusk!" says the woman, suddenly upset. "I don't drink! I'm a vegetarian!"

"No, not for *you*," says Peter, "for the *slugs*."

"Slugs like beer?" asks Johnny Kibble.

"A bit too much, I'm afraid. If you put a bowl full of beer in your garden, slugs will climb in overnight and drink until they're too drunk to climb out, and they drown."

"Any other questions?" asks Johnny Kibble. "Yes, the gentleman in the back."

"Yeah," says the gentleman in the back, "you look familiar. Didn't your used to be *Peter Vladiskovsky*, the mad scientist who did all those crazy transplant experiments?"

"Um…" says Peter nervously, "you must have me confused with someone else."

"Nope…never forget a face," says the gentleman in the back. "You transplanted the head of Dick Cheney onto the body of a human being."

An upset Peter stands up. "That was the *old* me! Don't judge me by my past!" he cries as he runs off stage.

∞

Back in his Madison, Wisconsin home, Peter is being comforted by his fiancé Annette Puddle, full-time student of real estate at Madison Community College.

On the kitchen table is a copy of that morning's *New York Times*, with the front-page headline: FORMER MAD SCIENTIST NOW LATE NIGHT SLUG SEXPERT.

"I've moved on in my life," says a distraught Peter, "but they keep dragging me back to my past. I've evolved as a person."

"If you've evolved as a person," says Annette while massaging Peter's shoulders, "then why are you letting this get to you?"

"Aren't you supposed to be comforting me, like the narrator said?"

"But honey, part of our relationship is speaking truth to each other."

"Want to have sex?"

"No. Check out the local newspaper. There's a big story about some sort of trouble over in Menomonie."

Peter gasps when he sees the headline: HORNY TEENS VANISH AFTER LOVER'S LANE RENDEZVOUS.

"Does the article give any clues about the incident that will require you to get involved?"

"Well, let's see…it says: 'Detectives were puzzled by the presence of massive quantities of…*Mucus!*'"

"You mean…mucus such as produced by a—"

"Yes, but it would have to be a tremendously big—"

"But is it possible that there could exist such a tremendously big—"

"I don't know for sure. So until I find out, we can't allow ourselves to finish our sentences. I better call up my brilliant colleague Dr. Poole from graduate school, who once allowed me to cover her with hot oil and ride her like a wild animal. I won't mention anything involving chocolate syrup."

"Okay. While you call up that skank I'm going outside to water the begonias and think about my future life as a real estate agent."

As Peter makes the call, he thinks to himself, *Wait a minute...I don't remember having begonias*. "Oh, hello! Is this Dr. Poole—I mean, *Jan?*...This is Peter—Peter *Mollusk*…That's right, chocolate syrup. Jan, did you hear about what happened in Menomonie? We suspect it might be a tremendously big—, but until we find out for sure we can't finish the sentence. So can you get out here right away?"

Peter decides to make another call.

"Hello, is this the United States Army?…This is Peter Mollusk, the nation's leading gastropodologist. I'm calling about the tragic accident that happened in Menomonie, Wisconsin. I have reason to believe that the horny teenagers were killed by a tremendously big–…That's right, a tremendously big–…I know that's hard to believe, but—"

Just then, from outside comes a woman's piercing scream.

"Annette! Is that you?"

Peter rushes outside to find Annette sprawled motionless on the lawn, next to a fallen ladder and a spilled can of paint. It looks like she'd been painting the window frames on the second floor. She must have fallen over and been knocked unconscious.

Then he notices something about her head. Something is unusual about the scene, something is a little "off."

Then he realized what's "off." It's her head! *It has been severed from her body!*

Struck silent by the horror of the sight, Peter falls to his knees. Then he falls to his shoulders. Then all the other parts of Peter that hadn't fallen to the ground fall, so they won't feel left out.

His mind races. *Annette! The woman I love! She is now head-less. Or body-less, depending on how you look at it. But no matter how you look at it, it doesn't look good.*

After Peter recovers from the shock, he notices a large piece of plate glass, covered with blood. Poor Jan! She must have accidentally knocked out the glass, then fallen on it. Well, at least it was over with quickly.

But wait, thinks Peter, *is it really over?*

He tears off his shirt and bundles up Annette's head. He runs into the house and downstairs toward the basement lab. *I can save her,* he thinks to himself.

Peter rushes into his basement lab. It's filled with bubbling test tubes, eerie mist produced by blocks of dry ice, and Tesla coils and Van de Graaff generators that look really cool.

In the lab is Kurt Linger—Peter's assistant from his old "mad scientist" days. Kurt refuses to leave the lab because of a botched attempt to replace a crushed hand with the only thing that was available. There's no easy way to say it: Kurt's left hand had been replaced with a *lobster claw.*

As Peter runs through the lab, Kurt is pouring red fluid into blue fluid.

"Purple!" says Kurt.

"Quickly, Kurt!" shouts Peter. "Prepare the formula!"

"Hey doc, what's in the bundle?" replies Kurt. "Maybe you found me a *left hand?*"

"Hurry, Kurt! Time is of the essence!"

"Jeez," says Kurt, attempting to guilt-trip Peter, "I try to make a little pleasant conversation and I get my head bitten off!" As Peter unwraps his bundle, Kurt spots its contents and adds, "Whoa! Talk about getting your head bitten off!"

"I'll explain later, but for now please prepare the nutritional formula."

"Oh God, I'm so lonely!" cries Kurt while pouring the formula into a shallow tray. "I need a woman to talk to, to shower with love and affection."

"Fortunately it was a nice clean cut," says Peter, placing Annette's head into the tray and taping electrodes behind her ears. "Kurt, are you ready with the oxygenator? I'll apply electrical current to jump-start her nervous system."

"Y'know, this is a delicate procedure," says Kurt, struggling with tubing, "and it would be helpful if I didn't have to do it with a *lobster claw*!"

"Haven't I apologized enough?"

"I'd trade all your apologies for something on the end of my left arm that doesn't have an exoskeleton."

Just then, Annette's head begins breathing.

"She's alive!" exclaims Peter.

Annette's head continues breathing, remaining unconscious, and begins mumbling. "Exterior trim…tasteful color scheme…important for salability…"

"Is she *dreaming?*"

"No, she's just reliving her last moments as an embodied head. She's stable for now, but I've got to find a donor body within 48 hours before deterioration begins."

"Why can't you just re-attach the head to her body?"

"Kurt, you know the answer! The transplant process only works with a living donor."

"I know that, of course, but the audience doesn't

know."

"Dang…48 hours to find a donor body and also investigate the incident in Menomonie about the possibility of a tremendously big—"

"While you're at it, would you keep your eyes open for a left hand? I'll never find a woman with this lobster claw, unless I find a woman who's seriously into crustacean kink. Of course, she'd also have to put up with my little quirks. For example, sometimes I get cravings for a big plate of sea urchins."

Just then Peter's cell phone rings.

"Peter Mollusk here…Oh, hello there General 'Buck' Turgidson from the United States Army… Oh, you're with the Special Forces Gastropod Defense Unit?…Yes, I can meet you at the Madison airport first thing in the morning."

"Kurt," says Peter, putting away his phone, "stay here and take good care of Annette, okay? If she regains consciousness, break the news to her gently. Please no jokes such as 'don't lose your head over it.'"

"It's always 'See you later, Kurt'! I hope Annette regains consciousness soon so I have somebody to talk to. At least *she* won't run off. Talk about a 'captive audience,' huh?"

"Gotta run!" says Peter.

∞

At the Moonlight Feels Right lounge in the Madison Regional Airport and Pancake House, Jan Poole—just in from Boston—is having a drink with Peter.

"Thank you, Jan, for coming out on such short notice. General 'Buck' Turgidson will be here soon to escort us to Menomonie."

"Oh, of course, Peter," chuckles Jan, "I'd do anything to save 'America's Dairyland'!"

"Please Jan, this is serious. Horny teenagers have been killed. And unless we figure out what caused it, more horny teenagers might be killed."

"Are you worried that Wisconsin will run out of horny teenagers?"

"Jan, please stop kidding around!"

"Peter, let's not talk about *horny teenagers*," Jan says seductively. "Let's talk about *chocolate syrup*. Do you remember that night? And the next night? And the next night? And the next night? And the—"

"Of course! How could I ever forget?"

"That night was very special to me. So was the next night. So was the next night. So was—"

"Jan, stop!" urges Peter. "You know that I'm engaged, right? Her name is Annette."

"Is Annette more sexually adventurous than me?"

"There's more to a relationship than—Oh! General 'Buck' Turgidson! General, how long have you been standing there?"

"Good afternoon, Mr. Mollusk. And you," he

adds, turning to Jan, "must be the brilliant Dr. Poole. I have a question: Did you use Hershey's or Nestlé's syrup?"

"Ghirardelli Black Label Chocolate Sauce," answers Jan, "the 64-ounce bottle with the individually purchased pump top."

"I have something important to tell you." says the general, his voice deepening into a serious military voice. "I'm afraid the entire population of Menomonie has totally vanished."

"Totally?" says Peter.

"Vanished?" adds Jan.

"Not a single person left. And the only evidence is that everything is covered with mucus. Slime trails everywhere! Up to twelve feet wide."

∞

In Peter's basement lab, Annette's head's eyes are moving behind closed lids as she mumbles randomly, "acceleration clause…fixed-rate mortgage… cost of funds index…merged credit report…"

"She's regaining consciousness!" shouts a delighted Kurt.

Annette's eyes open, and she looks around with mild surprise. "Kurt? Is that you? I feel kind of… *funny*. What happened to me?"

"I believe that hard news goes down easier with a laugh. So is it okay if I tell you with a series of jokes? First joke: What do you call a severed woman's head on a beach?"

"Huh? A severed woman's head on a beach? I give up."

"Sandy!"

"Oh, I see how it goes. Give me another one."

"What do you call a severed woman's head on a wire fence on a ranch?"

"Wire fence on a ranch? Oh—I know: *Barb!*"

"Yes!" says an excited Kurt. "Now you've got the hang of it. One more should do it, Annette. Here we go: What do you call a severed woman's head in the middle of a tennis court?"

"Oh, that's easy," laughs Annette. "It's Annette."

"That's right, Annette."

"Oh oh," says Annette's head with a blank look on her face.

Tentatively, Annette's head looks down, seeing nothing but a liquid-filled tray. "Oh, this won't do at all!"

"Annette, I have to say that you're taking this remarkably well. Perhaps it's because you have total confidence that your fiancé Peter will find a replacement body before your head begins deteriorating."

Producing a bottle, Kurt adds, "Hey, since Peter isn't here to boss me around, Doctor Kurt is in charge." Pouring some of the contents of the bottle into the nutritional formula, Kurt continues, "And Doctor Kurt prescribes a little *medicine* for his favorite patient. I hope you like tequila, Annette."

"As long as it's not that cheap *Jose Cuervo* junk. I only drink *Añejo* tequila with 100-percent blue agave."

"Wow, you really know your tequila!" says Kurt. Then he adds, while taking a swig from the bottle, "*And the good doctor prescribes a little medicine for himself.*"

As the doctor's medicine begins coursing through her bloodstream, Annette's head says, "Oh, that's good stuff! Is that *Reposado?*"

"Amazing!" exclaims Kurt, adding another splash.

"Hey Kurt," says Annette's head with a slight slur. "Have I ever told you about the importance of *staging* a house for a sale?"

"*Staging?* What's *that?*" answers Kurt, "And while you answer, *a little more medicine for the good doctor.*"

"Okay," slurs Annette's head. "Staging is what real estate agents do to make a house irresistible to the client."

"Are you talking about things like filling the home with the aroma of freshly-baked bread or cinnamon potpourris?"

"Oh, that's old school! People are wise to those cheap tricks by now."

"Wow, Annette, you really know your real estate!"

"I also need a refill. And don't be stingy with that bottle, Doc!"

∞

Peter, Jan, and General 'Buck' Turgidson walk along the deserted streets of downtown Menomonie.

"Whatever did this," the general says solemnly, "it did it last night. Does that fit the behavior of a —"

"Yes," replies Peter, "because *you-know-what's* are nocturnal. They must retreat to damp, dark hiding places during the day to avoid desiccation."

"I can relate," says the general. "I became desiccated once and it was a total bummer. I was in Copenhagen, getting drunk with a prostitute."

"Um…" says Peter. "*Getting drunk with a prostitute?* Are you allowed to say that?"

"Did I say, *getting drunk with a prostitute?*" says the general. "I meant to say, *smoking hash with a prostitute*."

Jan opens up a kit of scientific instruments, and makes scans with the spectrometer. Examining the readings, she says, "From these readings, I can confirm that the mucus is definitely *not* from a Republican. I'll know for sure after I check the calcium level."

"Excellent, Jan!" says Peter. "Then we'll know for sure that this mucus is definitely from a tremendously big—"

"SLUG!" shouts the general.

Crossing the Piggly Wiggly parking lot is a

tremendously big…*slug!*

"Well," says a relieved Peter, "at least now we can finish our sentences properly."

"I'm not scared," says General 'Buck' Turgidson, shakily pulling a pistol, "but I'm *pretending* to be scared to reassure you folks that it's okay."

"We're not scared," says Peter.

"But what if it sees us?" says the scared general.

"General," Jan offers, "the optical tentacles—the upper pair—merely sense the presence of light. The lower pair are *sensory* tentacles to detect smell, but we're downwind from the slug and are therefore undetectable."

"By the way, general," adds Peter, "either pair of tentacles can be re-grown if lost. Isn't that fascinating?"

"Hey general," adds Jan with a playful nudge, "I bet *you* can't re-grow a pair of lost tentacles!"

"Well, our course is clear," says the general, putting his pistol back in the holster. "I must order an all-out nuclear strike to destroy every living thing on earth."

"Um, general…?" offers Jan. "Wouldn't that, you know, also kill *us?*"

"Oh yeah," replies the General. "I'm open to other ideas. I'm also open to dating. Do either of you know any women with a thing for Generals?"

"I have an idea," offers Jan. "*Salt.*"

"Her name is *Salt?*" asks the General.

"No, General," clarifies Jan, "I'm talking about

actual *salt* – sodium chloride, common table salt which comes out of a salt shaker and adds zing to every meal."

"Salt kills slugs, General," adds Peter, "in addition to adding zing to every meal. It breaks down the protective mucus layer and dissolves the skin. The slug foams up and after it's all over all that's left is a little puddle of yuck."

"Well…" says General 'Buck' Turgidson, hesitantly, " I'll give your plan *12 hours* to work. But if the slugs are still alive after that, I'm authorizing Armageddon."

∞

In Peter's basement lab, Kurt is slouched sloppily on a chair. An empty glass is in his lobster claw. Annette's tray of nutritional formula includes an empty tequila bottle, several slices of lime, and a small toy boat.

"I'm outta shevered womin head jokesh," slurs Kurt. "How about shome shevered *man head* jokesh?"

"Hey Doctur Kurtish," says Annette's head, "I gotsh shome more *shtaging* advishe for ya! **hic** Oh dammit!"

More bubbles rise in the nutritional formula.

"Here'sh the firsht one," says Kurt. "What do ya callsh a shevered man's head hangin' ina musheum?"

"Oh that'sh eashy! *Art!* Hey Doctur Kurtish, wanna know how to shtage a home if the pershpective buyers are *hipshters?*"

"Annette, whatsh do you call a severed man'sh head under a bed?"

"Fill the fridge with PBR."

"No, it'sh *Dusty*. You're not even closhe! C'mon Annette, ushe your head!"

"Ha! What elshe am I gonna use? I like you, Kurt! You have a senshe of humor…unlike a shertain *fiancé* of mine. You're the cutesht guy with a lobshter claw I ever sheen!"

"And you are the funniesht shevered tequila-drinking womansh head I ever met!"

"I like bourbon, too. If I was shtaging a home for a horny shingle guy, I'd stash some naked *Hooters* waitresshes in the cupboards. Wait, shcratch that idea. Guysh never look in the cupboards."

"What do you call a shevered man's head laying nexsht to the front door?"

"But if it was a horny shingle *woman*, I'd fill the bathroom with *candlesh*. And I'd fill the bathtub with *Matthew McConaughey.*

"C'mon Annette! Here'sh a hint: It'sh rectangular an' you wipe your feetsh on it."

There is an urgent knocking at the door to the lab.

Peter's muffled voice shouts from the other side of the door. "Kurt! Are you there?"

<<< Peter bursts through the door, followed

closely by Jan who—upon viewing the scene—goes into a mild state of shock.

Peter spots Annette's head. "Annette! You're *conscious!*" Rushing over, he adds, "I want to give you a big hug, but I'm not sure how to hug a head."

Squinting her eyes, trying to get Peter into focus, Annette's head says, "Your voish is fermiliaar."

"Oh, Annette," pleads Peter, "don't you remember me, your fiancé?"

"Matt!" shouts Annette's head.

"Close," says Peter, "it's *Peter.*

"No, no…it'sh the puncshline to the *joke*. What do you call a shevered man's head laying nexsht to the front door? Matt!"

Just then, Peter notices the empty tequila bottles littering the lab, one of which was floating in Annette's nutritional formula.

Finally Jan has recomposed herself enough to say, "Hey, Peter? Not to intrude or anything, but what is going on here? And why does this Kurt guy have a crab claw for a hand?"

"It'sh not a crab!" yells an offended Kurt, "It'sh from a *lobshter!*"

"Settle down, Kurt," says Peter. Bringing Jan over to Annette's head, he says, "Jan, I would like to introduce you to the head of my fiancé, Annette."

Annette's head chuckles and says, "Hey, what do you call a shevered woman'sh head in the middle of a tennish court? The ansher ish *me*! Ha ha!"

"And Jan, you've already met my assistant, Kurt

Linger. Kurt assists me in my lab experiments."

"I'd shake yer hand," says Kurt, "excshept you probly don't wantsh to loshe any fingersh."

"Annette and Kurt," says Peter, "I'd like to introduce you to *Jan Poole*."

Annette's head eyes Jan suspiciously. "Hey… wait a shecond! Aren't you the one that had *shex* with my fiancé Matt?"

Jan turns to Peter. "Peter, I heard rumors that you did some 'unorthodox' experiments, but I never believed they were true!"

"Cheap husshy!" yells Annette's head.

"Honey?" says Peter to Annette's head. "I realize you might be a bit upset about losing your body, but I'm working on getting you a *brand new body.*"

"Peter?" says Jan, taking him aside. "This has me really worried about you. The line between scientific genius and obsessive fanaticism is a thin one. And I want you on the right side."

"No, you're wrong!" says Peter. "It's a wide fuzzy line, and I'm right on the edge of the middle of it. I'll get her another body. I'll make her complete again. And sober."

"But Peter," urges Jan. "Her drinking problem is an organic part of what she is. Also, her body. They co-evolved together: one body, one soul, one addiction. You can't just change her body to someone else's, or change her addiction to huffing paint thinner."

"I can!" says Peter, starting to sound a little too

much like a certain scientist in a certain 1931 movie directed by James Whale. "I can do it! I know I can."

Fortunately for Peter, or more accurately, fortunately for Peter's continuing denial, his cell phone suddenly rings. It's General 'Buck' Turgidson. "Hello general, any news?...*Really?*...You found all the giant slugs in the forest near *Oshkosh?... Hundreds* of them?...And you're not sure whether to refer to them as a *herd?*...No, general, that's a good guess but the term *gaggle* refers to a group of *geese*."

Jan says to Peter, "Peter, darling? I think the correct term for a bunch of slugs is: *a bunch of slugs*."

"Hey Jan," whispers Peter, "Please don't call me 'darling' in front of my fiancé's severed head." Into his phone, he says, "Oh, sorry general—I was talking to Doctor Poole."

Finished with his phone call, Peter announces: "The fate of the entire world hangs in the balance. We have less than 36 hours to stop the slugs before the general triggers nuclear orgasm."

"You mean *Armageddon*," interrupts Jan.

"I'm afraid that General 'Buck' Turgidson sees total nuclear destruction as the ultimate orgasm."

∞

The next morning, Peter and Jan join General

'Buck' Turgidson in his jeep, as he heads up the slopes of Mount Oshkosh.

"We set up a temporary command center on the summit," explains the general. "The slugs are due any minute now." The general hands Peter a manila envelope. "This contains high-resolution reconnaissance photos from one of our spy planes. These photos show that we're now dealing with *thousands* of giant slugs."

Examining the photos, Peter says, "Actually, general, these are nude photos of Emma Watson."

"What?!" shouts the general. "These must be from one of those 'celebrity fake' websites. Look at this one: The skin tone doesn't even match. It looks like Emma's head has been severed and stuck on another body."

Peter flinches.

"What's wrong?" says the general. "Don't you find Emma Watson attractive?"

"Hey!" shouts Jan. "The bomber is here!"

Above them, a B-52 Stratofortress comes into view. It struggles to retain elevation, due to carrying an immense salt shaker nearly as large as the bomber itself. The shaker is mounted beneath the bomber on an immense hinge, with a massive steel cable looped around the top and leading to a huge winch.

The ground begins rumbling, and in the distance can be heard really disgusting "slurping" sounds. A seething, slithering mass of thousands of tremendously big slugs tears steadily through the forest. Large pine trees fall like toothpicks, macerated by the slugs with their radulas. Then the slug army leaves the woods and begins crossing a farm field.

"Perfect!" says General 'Buck' Turgidson. "We've got them out in the open! Excuse me, I need to get on my combat radio to communicate with the bomber pilot."

GENERAL: "Hello? Is this Lieutenant...*Rostovo...Rostrosev...Rostapasta...*"

LIEUTENANT: "It's Rostrovopichinsky, sir—but you can call me *Moe*. Over."

GENERAL: "I appreciate that, Moe. Are you all set up there? Over."

LIEUTENANT: "Affirmative, general. Major Baker is at the winch, ready to hit the switch at your command. Over."

GENERAL: "Excellent! Prepare for the attack. When I give the word, Moe flies low and Baker lowers the shaker. Over."

LIEUTENANT: "We're ready, general. Over."

GENERAL: "Not quite…not quite…Okay: *The Word!*"

Major Baker hits the switch, and the immense winch chugs to life and the massive shaker begins lowering. Just as the salt begins pouring out of the shaker, the huge metal cap…*falls off.* It tumbles through the air, then smashes into the ground, followed closely by 100 tons of salt, landing right in front of the slugs in a mountainous white glop.

The lead slug, unable to stop its tremendous momentum in time to avoid the salt, plunges straight into it. It begins quivering, then its entire body erupts into sizzling foam.

"It's working, general!" exclaims Peter. "We've confirmed that salt kills them, in addition to adding zing to every meal. We need to re-load another shaker, except this time tighten the cap."

"Wait a minute," says Jan, "something's happening."

Suddenly, the lead slug stops foaming and rises high into the air, its foot solidly anchored by its massive foot fringe.

"It's *mutating*," shouts Jan, "right before our eyes! Whatever we devise to kill them, they'll just rapidly mutate the ability to tolerate it!"

General 'Buck' Turgidson clasps his hands in delight. "Oh boy! It's just a matter of time before I can shoot my missiles!"

"General!" says Jan. "We have a deal! We have another six hours before you give those missiles a hand job."

"C'mon, Jan!" says Peter. "The slugs are headed toward Milwaukee. We've got to get there and find a way to stop them!"

Just then Peter's cell phone rings.

"Peter Mollusk here...Oh, it's you, Kurt... You're calling about *who?*...Oh, *Annette*...No, I haven't forgotten. But just between you and me, Kurt, I'm unsure whether she's been doing her share of the growth in our relationship…No, I haven't found her a body yet, but it's definitely on my to-do list. Don't worry about a… Hello?…Hello?…"

∞

In Peter's basement lab, an angry Kurt is staring at his cell phone.

Annette's head says, "What was that about, Kurt honey?"

"Kurt honey doesn't think that your fiancé gives a rip whether you get a new body. Wait a sec…what did you call me? Kurt *honey?*"

"Kurt honey, I'm really sleepy. I think I'm going to take a nap."

"That's fine, Annette. You get some rest while Kurt honey takes matters into his own hands."

Kurt adds quietly to himself, *"Even if one of those hands is a claw."*

Annette's head is blissfully snoring as Kurt continues talking to himself. "We're running out of time. And Peter is *not* going to help me. He's going to leave Annette for that skank Jan!"

He gazes lovingly upon Annette's snoring head. "Well, Annette, I want you to know that *somebody* loves you…*somebody* cares. Sleep soundly, dear Annette, while I go find you a new body!"

He kisses Annette's head gently on the forehead,

and heads upstairs out of the basement. While making his way out of the house, Kurt notices a platypus waddling across the lawn.

"That's strange," he says. "What's a semi-aquatic mammal endemic to eastern Australia doing in central Wisconsin?"

The platypus—unconcerned with such questions—smiles at Kurt with its rubbery duck-billed snout. It wags its beaver-like tail and scuttles about on its short otter-like webbed feet.

Kurt mutters to himself, "Sorry Annette, but there's no time to be picky."

Suddenly the platypus is beneath an immense shadow. When it looks up, it's shocked to see Kurt hovering overhead and tossing a net over it.

∞

Peter and Jan are in downtown Milwaukee, walking along Prospect Avenue overlooking Lake Michigan.

Jan is reading the *Milwaukee Journal Sentinel*, with the front-page headline: MILWAUKEE EVACUATES AS GIANT SLUGS APPROACH.

Reading aloud from the text of the article, Jan says, "Scientists Peter Mollusk and Jan Poole are engaged in a futile effort to stop the slugs before General 'Buck' Turgidson launches all-out nuclear Armageddon."

Jan turns to Peter in despair. "Peter, what can we

do to be non-futile?"

Peter and Jan continue their walk, entering Veteran's Park while scratching their heads, gazing skyward, holding their chins in their hands, and other gestures to indicate they are deep in thought.

"This isn't working," says Jan. "There must be other gestures—more *extreme* gestures. Hey, how about the pose in that famous statue *The Thinker* by Auguste Rodin?"

"I'm willing to try anything at this point!" he says, hopping on a boulder. "Let's see…sitting on a boulder with head bowed and resting on my upturned arm. Hey Jan, does this look right?"

"That looks right, except in the sculpture the figure is naked. Now Peter, I know you're shy about your body, but… Oh, your clothes are off already."

"Hey, this feels *great!* So liberating! For the first time in my life, I feel *free!*" Standing up and raising his arms, Peter adds, "Look, Jan, I'm a golden eagle!"

An elderly woman approaches Peter. "Excuse me, are you Peter Mollusk, the world-famous gastro-podologist? I just wanted to thank you for helping me out with my garden problem."

Peter stops flapping his arms and answers, "Huh? What garden problem?"

"Don't you recognize me? From *The Late Night Talk Show with Johnny Kibble*," she said, showing him her seed packets and watering can.

"Excuse me, ma'am," says Jan, "but we're pretty busy figuring out a way to defeat the giant slugs."

"Well," she says, "Mr. Mollusk's advice sure solved *my* slug problem!"

"Advice?" asks Jan.

"Yes. Mr. Mollusk suggested I try—"

"Beer!" shouts Peter, suddenly remembering.

"Worked like a charm! I set out a bowl of beer, and in the morning it was full of slugs with their radulas sticking out and goofy smiles on their pneumostomes."

Jan blurts out, "Peter! Are you thinking what I'm thinking?"

"Yes! I should start a gardening advice column!"

"No, Peter! It's our chance to defeat the tremendously big slugs!"

"I decided," says the woman, "that when my time is up that's how I'm gonna go. Just fill up the bathtub with Budweiser and leave this world as happy as a slug."

"Luckily," says Peter, "we're in Milwaukee—beer-brewing capitol of the country."

"But where are we going to put all the beer?"

The woman gazes into the distance and says, "Isn't it beautiful how the sun is shining on *Lake Michigan?*"

"I have an idea!" says Peter. "We'll fill Lake Michigan with Milwaukee's finest. But we'll have to get rid of the water first. We've got to contact the Port Authority! Tell them to open all the spillways."

"There's no time!" yells Jan. "The Lake Michigan basin contains 1,180 cubic miles of water, and it would take *weeks* to drain."

"Excuse me," says the woman, "I just thought I'd mention that a 10-megaton nuclear blast at a depth of 200 fathoms will vaporize 1,180 cubic miles of water. Of course, you'd need access to a 10-megaton nuclear device."

Peter and Jan look at each other and yell simultaneously, "General 'Buck' Turgidson!"

Within seconds, Peter is on his cell phone. "Yes, general, we have a plan. Order every brewery in Milwaukee to produce at full capacity, ready to release into Lake Michigan at my command. Second—you're going to *love* this part—we need you to order a nuclear strike ASAP…No, a *limited* strike, just one warhead: A 10-megaton device set to detonate at 200 fathoms just offshore from downtown Milwaukee…Yes, general—right now would be just fine…Yes, I know you're excited. Goodbye, general."

Peter ends the call and looks thoughtfully into the sky.

"Well Jan," he says, "get ready to watch a hell of a show."

"Peter," she replies, "you should really put your clothes back on."

∞

Just north of downtown Milwaukee at McKinley Park, all is silent but for the pleasant whistling of birds and the soothing chirping of two non-conformist crickets.

The camera pans from the clear blue sky down to a parking lot which Milwaukee teens refer to as "a parking lot."

Parked there are two horny Wisconsin teenagers in a blue 1965 Mustang convertible.

"Hey Brenda-Lou," says Johnny, "let's go all the way."

"Gosh, I don't know," says Brenda-Lou. "I've got to think about the *future*."

Just then, an immense explosion on Lake Michigan cause Johnny and Brenda-Lou to cover their eyes and duck under the dashboard. When they emerge, a shimmering mushroom cloud steadily expands high into the stratosphere.

"Oh my God!" cries Johnny.

"They did it!" says a stunned Brenda-Lou. "I can't believe they actually did it!"

"Did *what?*"

"The bomb," says Brenda-Lou, starting to cry. "The *nuclear* bomb. That crazy general actually went through with it. There's nothing to live for now. We have no future."

"Hey," smiles Johnny, "that's *great!*"

"*What???*"

"Well, if there's no future, then we might as well go all the way!"

“Mom always told me that guys have a one track mind!” protests Brenda-Lou. She turns once again to watch the rising mushroom cloud, then says, “Oh, what the heck. Let’s get it over with.”

∞

The tremendously huge slugs surge into outer Milwaukee, leaving a trail of broken dreams and a lot of mucus.

TOTALLY GROSS, screams the front-page headline of the afternoon edition of the *Milwaukee Journal Sentinel.*

The streets of Milwaukee are filled with panicked people running amuck. Far from the chaos are Peter and Jan. They watch as the mushroom cloud gradually dissipates, leaving a Lake Michigan basin that’s bone dry.

“It worked!” says Jan.

Peter is on his phone. “General, it’s Peter Mollusk…Yes, general it made a really big ‘boom’… General, listen to me: Alert all Milwaukee breweries to start pumping everything they’ve got into the big crater, okay? Talk to you later, general.”

“We’re in luck, Peter. There’s a strong east wind, which will send the aroma of beer right to the slugs.”

“Excellent!”

“Peter, this would probably be a good time for you to put your clothes on.”

As Peter continues to not put his clothes on, the collective breweries of Milwaukee are pumping millions of gallons of frothy goodness to the lakeshore, and forming the world's biggest bowl of beer.

"Just in time, narrator," says Peter, "because *here come the slugs!*"

The slugs squeeze through the glass-walled streets of downtown Milwaukee, sliming all over each other in a mad frenzy.

"It's working!" shouts Jan. "They're crazy for the beer!"

But at that exact moment, the strong east wind suddenly stops. The air becomes dead calm. The slugs begin to disperse back into downtown Milwaukee to continue their reign of death and terror and really disgusting "slurping" sounds.

"Oh no!" cries Peter. "It's all over. We're witnessing the beginning of an era that will signal the start of an epoch that will mean the total annihilation of humankind."

"That's too melodramatic!" says Jan. "Nobody will take that line seriously. How about just saying that we're *doomed?"*

"Okay," says Peter. "My career as an actor is doomed."

"No, Peter! *Humanity* is doomed."

"Oh yeah, them too"

"Not *yet* it is!" shouts a slightly-drunk male voice. "*Doomed*, I mean. *Humanity*, that is. **hic**

Oh heck, can I start over?"

Peter spins around to see that the slightly-drunk male voice is coming from….

"Kurt!" shouts a shocked Peter. "What are you doing here? And what are you doing with a *platypus*?"

The head attached to the platypus says, with a slight slur, "Whatsch the matter, Peter? Don't you recognize your *fiancé?*"

Peter is struck speechless by the sight of Annette's head on a platypus body

"This is really interesting," says Jan, "but shouldn't we be doing something about the blob-like army of giant slugs that are no longer heading toward the beer?"

Annette looks up toward Jan and says, "Oh, we'll take care of those nasty 'ol slugs, won't we dear."

"We came here to volunteer for a suicide mission," says Kurt. "We are prepared to give our lives some meaning by sacrificing ourselves to save humanity."

"But *how?*" asks Jan.

"With this case of Budweiser," says Kurt. Taking out a can, he majestically shakes it up then snips off the top with his lobster claw, sending a spray of beery foam in the direction of the giant slugs. Walking toward the slugs, he says, "Here, sluggy-slug-slugs! Get your nice beer here!"

Annette turns to walk beside Kurt, splashing her

otter-like webbed feet in the trail of beery puddles left by Kurt. "Here, sluggy-slugs!"

The lead slug perks up, its sensory tentacles extending to get a whiff of its favorite beverage. Then a few other slugs do likewise.

"We got their attention!" says Annette.

"Fantastic," says Kurt, cont-inuing to spray cans of beer at them. "Now, let's lead them to the crater."

The lead slug tentatively follows Kurt and Annette out to the lakeshore. Then the hundreds of other giant slugs follow.

Peter and Jan hold each other as Kurt and Annette disappear into the beer-filled crater, followed closely by the slugs. As the slug mass slowly sinks beneath the surface, there is a bit of sudsy bubbling. Then all is quiet.

The suspense is unbearable as Peter and Jan wait to see if the beer will have the desired effect. There's a full minute of really melodramatic music, which finally fades away.

"So it seems…" Peter offers tentatively, "that humanity is saved?"

"Thanks to Kurt and Annette," says Jan, with a tear in her eye. "They made the ultimate sacrifice."

"Yes, they really took one for the team," says Peter, as melodramatically as possible. *"They took one for Team Humanity."*

Thoroughly satisfied with his performance and imagining the theater audience rising to give a standing ovation, Peter pauses to wait for the applause to die down while composing his Oscar acceptance speech. Then he ponders his chances of winning a Best Actor award for a movie that includes a severed head with a drinking problem.

"That means we can finally relax," says Jan. "It's probably about time for you to put your clothes back on."

"I was thinking," says Peter with a playful smirk, "that it's probably about time for *you* to take your clothes *off*."

∞

Back at McKinley Park, a naked Johnny and Brenda-Lou are relaxing in the blue 1965 Mustang convertible. Brenda-Lou is experiencing post-coital bliss. Johnny is not.

"Well, it looks like Armageddon didn't quite happen," says Johnny.

"I suppose I should be mad at you for tricking me," says a smiling Brenda-Lou. "I mean, the world didn't end. But my *own* world sure got rocked! I felt as if my inner being opened up to the entire universe, as if some essential aspect of my own soul briefly touched what Emerson described as the 'Over-Soul'—the aspect of eternity alive in us all yet which we rarely experience in full splendor. In other words, I think I had an orgasm."

Just then, a red 1965 Mustang convertible pulls up next to Johnny and Brenda-Lou.

In the front seat of the red Mustang are a naked Peter and Jan next to a 64-ounce bottle of Ghirardelli Black Label Chocolate Sauce with the individually purchased pump top.

"Hey there, horny Wisconsin teenagers," shouts Peter, "do you mind if we party next to you?"

"No problem!" says Brenda-Lou. "Hey, Johnny just helped me have my first orgasm!"

∞

As the sun sets, the camera pans to a front view of two side-by-side 1965 Mustang convertibles with four naked horny people behind the windshields. As they begin breathing heavily and slowly descend out of view, the camera pans up to the beautiful sunset sky as the end credits begin scrolling down the screen

Normally, movies like this end with screams of terror, but this one ends with screams of ecstasy. That's what you get for ending a movie with four naked horny people in two 1965 Mustang convertibles.

~ ~ ~

THE FAMOUS VAUGHN BROTHERS APOCALYPTIC MATINEE AND SUPER DEATH FREAK-OUT SHOW

BY: RUSSELL HOLBROOK

The old wood of the antique chair creaked as Jeff leaned back and lit his cigar. Quasimodo adjusted himself in his chair across the small café' table, leaned forward, and ripped a fart that spanked the ancient wood under his wide ass and echoed through the coffee shop. Jeff wrinkled his nose and blew out a puff of blue smoke.

"Geez, Quasi, what the hell?"

"Sorry buddy, it must be the fourteen blocks of extra-sharp cheddar cheese I had for breakfast."

"Cheese makes you fart?"

"Yeah, it, uh..." Quasimodo squeezed his eyes and another fart that sounded like a cross between a screaming hamster and shredding cloth rippled against his chair. He squealed in discomfort as the noxious emission tore out of his ass.

One of the café's baristas approached the table.

"Hey you guys, not to be a dick, but, there's no farting allowed in here. You're gonna have to take that outside." As he spoke, the barista pointed to a sign hanging on the wall which featured a crude drawing of a stick figure passing gas, surrounded by a bright red circle with a line through it. The words "Absolutely No Farting Allowed" were printed in bold black letters beneath the drawing.

Jeff blew out a massive cloud of cigar smoke and shrugged his shoulders.

Quasimodo shook his head and got up from his chair, spreading rank fumes around the table. "Ugh… I'll be back in a few minutes…I hope."

Jeff gripped his nose with one hand and gave Quasimodo the thumbs up. His friend left the table and headed for the door. The barista nodded to Jeff and slouched back to his station behind the coffee bar.

Jeff reached into his messenger bag and brought out a worn spiral bound notebook. He flipped it open and smiled. His new story was coming along so well that it almost worried him. If he kept up his current pace and momentum, his story could turn into a monster Horror novel.

"Ah, my sweet baby," Jeff said to himself as he flipped through the most recent pages.

Jeff had started the Awesome Authors of Super Scary Stories writers group so like-minded writers who were fed up with the mainstream fiction scene could get together once a week and hang out, bounce ideas off each other, offer helpful criticism and advice, and, most of all, encourage each other in their shared dream of writing a story so scary, so diabolical, that it would destroy the world. Jeff's eyes scanned through his story as he awaited the arrival of his fellow writers.

The bell attached to the front door jingled. Jeff looked up to see Vic Frankenstein walking in, followed by his seven and a half foot tall, green, sewn together son, Vic Jr.

"Franky…!" Jeff called out, a huge smile pasted across his face.

"Jeffery, please, call me Vic. You know how I detest that crude, pedestrian nickname," Vic said.

A huge laugh burst out of Jeff. "Okay, buddy."

Vic and Vic Jr. each took a seat.

"Why'd ya bring Vic Jr.?" Jeff asked.

"Vamparilla had a dentist's appointment so she couldn't watch him. I do hope that you don't mind that I brought him. He has been working passionately on his own non-fiction writing; a dissertation on why fire should be outlawed."

At the mention of fire, Vic Jr. jumped in his seat and let out a small roar. "Now, now…don't be frightened." Vic Sr. patted his son on the shoulder and Vic Jr. relaxed and nestled back into his seat.

"Jeffery," Vic began, "Quasimodo is outside making horrible, anguished facial expressions and is exuding the most pungent odors. Is he ill?"

Jeff smirked. "Yeah, you could say that. He said

he ate too much cheese."

"Ah, yes, lactose intolerance, an affliction which affects many... Will he be joining us?"

"Yeah, just as soon as he, um, gets it all out."

"Very well," Vic Sr. said, "I am very eager for our discussion to begin as I feel I have made great strides since our meeting last."

Looking at his watch, a look of concern swept over Jeff's face. "Have you heard from Jekyll and Hyde? They're usually here by now."

"Oh dear, I thought you already knew," Vic Sr. said, wringing his hands. Vic Jr. groaned and shook his head.

"Knew what...?" Jeff asked.

"Jekyll and Hyde parted ways."

"What...?! They're getting a divorce?!"

"Yes, dear Jeffery, I'm afraid so. Poor Jekyll is in absolute hysterics and Hyde is on a rampage. I heard just this morning that he was seen drunk and carousing on the boulevard into the wee hours all weekend."

"Well, you know, Vic, we each deal with grief in our own way. I'm sure it's tough on 'em both. This is terrible!"

"Indeed, it truly is. I did speak briefly with Jekyll last evening; he said he would attend today in an effort to brighten his cheerless heart. However, I would not anticipate his arrival with any sincere hope."

"I always have hope, Vic, and I wanna keep my

eyes peeled just in case either of those two shows up."

"In that case, it's a good thing that I brought my Vaughn Brothers Eye Peeler, patent pending. 'Vaughn Brothers, a name you can trust!'" Vic Frankenstein plopped his black medicine bag on the table and began furiously rummaging through its contents. "Ah yes, here we are!" He said triumphantly as he pulled out what looked like a potato peeler with a calculator watch attached to it. "This wonderful device will give you incredible depth of extra-sensory sight, Jeffery. Surely, if either Jekyll or Hyde makes an appearance, you will see them most clearly!"

After calibrating the Eye Peeler to work with Jeff's eyes, he handed the device to Jeff and went to the bar to order a quintuple espresso.

Jeff peeled his eyes and looked around. He took a puff off his cigar. "Holy wow! I've never been able to see like this before. Everything is so clear and beautiful!"

A sudden roar came from outside the café'. A woman screamed and the coffee shop door blew in with such force that it slammed against the wall, knocking down a framed, signed photo of Dracula. Quasimodo walked in, smiling. Jeff saw vapor trails that sparkled like they were made of diamonds following Quasimodo as he made his way to the group's table.

"Hey Q, you're farts are sparkly!" Jeff shouted

with wonder.

"Awesome," Quasimodo said with a smile, "I always thought there was something special about me, besides my ginormous hunch back and my crazy eye."

Just as Quasimodo was getting settled into his seat, Jekyll flew through the door with a hulking typed manuscript under his arm.

"I've done it! I've done it!" Jekyll hollered from across the room, "I've created a story so mad with Horror, so grim and obscene, so foul with evil, that no one who reads it can retain their sanity! Muwahahaha!"

Jekyll slammed the massive manuscript down on the table, shaking Jeff's coffee cup.

"Goddammit men, somebody get me a latte!" Jekyll screamed, turning toward the bar. "Barkeep!"

Vic Jr. moaned again and put his face in his hands. Vic Sr. said hi to Jekyll as the frantic man passed him by on his way to the bar. Vic sat back down next to Jeff and sipped his espresso. "Aaahhh perfection in a cup," He motioned to the large stack of papers in the center of the table. "I take it that's Jekyll's so-called masterpiece?"

Jeff nodded. "Yep,the one and only," Jeff peered at the unbound book. His peeled eyes drew a sharp focus on the disheveled mound of off-white paper. The top pages ruffled as if by a quiet breeze. Jeff's brow wrinkled. The manuscript bounced. "What the…?" Jeff whispered.

The pages started to shake. A rumbling sound came from the bottom of the stack. Vic Sr. stopped sipping his espresso. His eyes thinned and he leaned forward. Vic Jr. got up, left the table with a groan, and headed for the men's room.

The table began to vibrate. Jeff stared at Jekyll's manuscript with his wide, peeled eyes as it started shaking violently.

"What the deuce?" Vic Sr. shouted. He turned in his chair and yelled: "Jekyll! Your manuscript is displaying quite an odd temperament."

Jekyll threw his latte' at the barista, nailing the poor guy on the bridge of the nose, and ran back to the table.

"What in Satan's name are you doing to my manuscript?" Jekyll said to Jeff in a voice of high-pitched agitation.

"Nothing, J, I was just looking at it and it started shaking and bouncing," Jeff replied.

The table went from vibrate to shake.

"Calm down, Percy, daddy's here," Jekyll said to his book. The book rumbled and hopped.

Vic's eyes shot out wide. "It's alive! It's alive!" He cackled.

"You made him upset!" Jekyll yelled, pointing a long, boney finger at Jeff. "He's self-conscious enough as it is, and you had to go looking at him with your second sight!"

"Whoa, buddy…Nobody said anything about second sight…"

"Everyone knows that the Vaughn Brother's Eye Peeler gives you second sight. Other known side-effects are prophecy and leaky bowel syndrome."

Jeff cut his eyes at Vic Sr., who shrugged his shoulders and smiled.

"Damn you, Jeffery!" Jekyll continued. "If he doesn't calm down, he's going to fall apart and spill out everywhere!"

"Jekyll, buddy, I swear I didn't mean to- wait, you named your manuscript Percy? What kind of name-"

"It's a family name!" Jekyll screamed in hysteria.

Now everyone in the crowded café' was staring at Percy the manuscript, making it more and more nervous. A high, nasally cry burst out of the center of the stack of pages. Plates and cups rattled and shook behind the coffee bar.

"Percy, no!" Jekyll shrieked. "Calm down! It's alright, it's alright, it's-"

But it was too late. Percy's cry turned into a horrid wail. Plates and cups and glasses exploded. Glass and porcelain shot into the barista's eyes. Percy cried even louder.

Jeff couldn't look away. The pages all started spinning round and round, faster and faster, as if in an invisible vortex. The words started flying off Percy's pages, hurling themselves through the air, stabbing the café' guests and burrowing into their flesh.! Blood poured out of the screaming coffee drinkers. They fell to the floor, writhing in agony.

A paragraph went spinning after a hipster, slicing his neck and sending his head bouncing off and rolling across the floor. A fleeing step-father, whose eyes had been gouged out by action verbs stepped on the severed hipster head, slipped, and got impaled on one of Jekyll's overly descriptive, tender ruminations on the nature of cyclic passing of the lycanthropy gene from generation to generation with the possible interruption of said cycle and the possibility thereof [SIC].

A paroxysm arose from across the coffee shop as Quasimodo blew out a huge fart and blew out one of the shop's front windows, exploding glass onto the sidewalk and injuring several pedestrians. Jeff watched the fart propulsion in awe, Quasimodo's gas taking on the form of fire from a rocket ship.

Jeff puffed on his cigar and watched more and more words stream out of Jekyll's spinning manuscript. The words filled the café', severing limbs, slicing throats and painting the floor, the tables, and the walls with blood. Destroying costly merchandise, killing dreams, and gorging and gutting the helpless coffee shop patrons.

Vic Jr. sat on the toilet, listening to the pandemonium taking place on the other side of the bathroom wall. He sighed and rested his chin in his hand. *Blah-bi-da-di-blag-blud-dar-ga-mek-ka-dooo-eee-la*, he thought to himself.

Vic Sr. leaned back in his chair, lit a cigarette, took another sip of his espresso, and smiled at the carnage around him. "Now this is what I call a Tuesday.!"

"I couldn't agree more, my friend. Cheers!" Jeff said, raising his coffee mug to Vic's.

The two friends each took a sip of their drinks and a puff off their smokes.

"Percy! For the love of Criminy, please stop!" Jekyll shouted over the roar of screaming and smashing that filled the café'.

Percy the manuscript spun faster and faster, becoming a black and off-white blur until he screeched to an abrupt halt.

Percy's title page shot out and flew across the room, slicing off an old woman's scalp as it spun through the air. With an ear-shattering squeal the title page collided with the street side wall of the coffee shop. The wall exploded onto the sidewalk. Bricks and mortar rained down on the busy street and sidewalk, smashing windshields, windows, and pedestrian's faces.

Drivers shit their pants in terror, surprise, and fury. They were already upside down in their stupid car loans, and now this!

The motorists swerved to avoid the exploding wall. Head on collisions clogged the road. The traffic stood still. All the drivers started honking and screaming and cursing. Drooling, their eyes red with hate, the swearing motorists looked around for someone to blame. At that exact moment, Jeff, Jekyll, and Vic Frankenstein and his son, who had finally come out of the bathroom, strolled out of the gaping hole in the side of the café', sipping and smoking and observing the chaos. Quasimodo spotted them and ran to their side.

"Wow, you guys, this is amazing!" Jeff exclaimed. He turned to Jekyll. "You did it, J! Your book is destroying the world!" Jeff's face filled with awe and pride. "I'm so proud of you!"

Tears filled Jekyll's eyes. He sighed. "Aye yet this, my greatest achievement, the culmination of my life's ambitions, feels so empty without my soul mate, my dearest friend, my most beloved rump ranger, my most expeditious butt pirate, my sweet, sweet Hyde."

Jeff saw the dark sadness covering Jekyll, taking away his light.

All the friends felt their hearts break for Jekyll. A child passed them on the sidewalk, running and screaming for his mother.

"We're here, Jekyll, and we love you," Quasimodo said.

"Yeah, buddy, we love you. And this is a great moment for us all," Jeff said. "Besides, who knows, maybe Hyde will come to his senses, realize what he's missing, and come back to you."

Jekyll nodded. "One can only hope."

"Yeah, I'm sure he'll-…" A sharp elbow nailed Jeff in the ribs and stopped his would-be encouraging speech. The throng of disfigured café' guests were stampeding out onto the sidewalk soaked in guts, snot, and blood.

Vic's eyes burst wide. "It's the caffeine! It's kept them alive and sent them on a blood-thirsty rampage!"

The Awesome Authors of Super Scary Stories stepped out of the way as the group of caffeinated maniacs ran out into the clogged street.

The drivers with their crashed cars, still searching for a scapegoat for their discomfort, saw Jeff and his friends smiling and watching the horde flowing out of the café'. They saw Jeff's wide, peeled eyes and they knew he had the extra vision. The motorists' anger grew. They bared their teeth and snarled.

"It's *his* fault, the one with the extra sight!" A woman trapped in a burning car screamed, pointing her finger at Jeff. "It's him! Him, him, him…!"

All the eyes of the motorists turned and beamed their laser hate at Jeff. And Jeff saw their hate as a bright red, consuming fire.

"Oh shit!" Jeff yelled. He turned to his friends. "They think the traffic jam is my fault because I have such awesome eyes.!"

"Kill the freaks, they did this to us! This is all because of them!" A blood covered preppy boy screamed as he climbed out of his smashed beamer.

The mob in the street joined forces with the caffeinated maniacs and started skulking toward Jeff and his friends.

"Now they're blaming all of us!" Quasimodo screeched.

Vic Jr. groaned and slapped his massive hand on his forehead.

"To the castle…!" Vic Sr. shouted, pointing in the direction of the castle.

Quasimodo turned around and faced his back to the crowd. "You guys go on ahead; I'll hold 'em off."

"But my dear Quasimodo…" Jekyll began.

"Go on, I'll catch up," Quasimodo insisted.

The crowd grew closer.

"Run…!" Jeff screamed. He beamed an enraged middle school teacher in the head with his coffee mug and the friends took off, running for the castle.

The mob surged forward. Quasimodo bent over and concentrated. Right as the mob was on him he squeezed and a machine gun line of high-velocity farts shot out of his ass, pulverizing the front line of the vicious crowd. Exploding flesh from heads and limbs and torsos filled the air, showering the street with gore. Quasimodo squeezed out another round and the second line of the mob exploded into tiny fleshy bits.

All the blood and exploded flesh seemed to only fuel the mob's quest for vengeance. Quasimodo squeezed again but he was all out of farts. The furious mob charged forward. And Quasimodo ran for his life.

☺

When Quasimodo caught first glimpse of his friends, they were running along the winding path that led up to the castle.

"Heeeyyy yooouuu guuuyyysss…!" Quasimodo shouted.

Jeff looked back and saw Quasimodo with the mob hot on his heels. Jeff swept his hand forward, telling his friend to step it up. Quasimodo ran as fast as he could. His extra effort pushed out an unexpected stress fart. The sudden burst of butt gas rocketed Quasimodo through the air. He spread his arms wide and flew up the path, over a turn, across the ravine filled with deadly, deadly vipers, and landed on the path next to Jeff. The two buddies smiled and patted each other on the back. And they ran.

As the group neared the castle, Vic Sr. pulled out the drawbridge remote. He thumbed the button and prayed that the bridge would be down by the time they reached the moat. With a loud groan, the archaic bridge began to lower. The mob gained more and more ground, screaming out their lust for death.

The drawbridge touched down just as the writers were mere inches from the moat. Jeff shouted in triumph when his feet landed on the aged boards. The band of friends tore across the bridge to the castle's gigantic garage doors. Vic Sr. frantically searched his pockets for the garage door remote.

Jekyll looked out over the moat and saw the mob beginning to come up the last hill leading up to the castle. His heart went into double time. "Make haste, Victor! The haters are nearly upon us!"

"I'm searching with all the speed at my behest!" Vic Sr. replied as lint, coins, and jelly beans flew out of his pockets.

"Instead of having two remotes, why not just get a universal remote and then you'll only have one?" Jeff asked.

"Jeffery! I…" Vic Sr. began.

"Reeaahhh…" Vic Jr. said, nudging his father's arm.

Vic Sr. looked up to see his son holding out a remote and smirking.

"Oh, bless you my dear boy!" Vic Sr. exclaimed.

Taking the remote from his son, the glad father kissed Vic Jr. on the cheek. He hit the button and the garage doors groaned and began to rise.

"Vic, raise the bridge!" Jeff yelled.

Vic Sr. punched the button on the drawbridge remote. Like a hundred year old billionaire who's Viagra has just kicked in, the drawbridge slowly began to lift off the ground. And then it stopped. Vic Sr. punched the button again, and again.

"Damn this twentieth century technology!" Vic Sr. yelled as he punched the button again.

Jeff saw the faces of the mob coming up over

the top of the hill. "Hurry, Vic! They're almost here!"

"I'm trying, Jeffery, I'm trying!" Vic Sr. shook the remote and pressed the button again. There was a click and the bridge started another ascent.

"Yes!" Jeff shouted. Quasimodo cheered and clapped. Everyone felt a sense of relief, except for Jekyll. He moved forward. His eyes narrowed as he peered into the storming mob, watching, listening. He thought he heard a most familiar voice, a voice that had cried out his name innumerable times in the deep of night, a voice that he loved more than any other in the wide world.

"Jeeekkyyllll…!" The voice cried out, soaring over the mob's cacophonous roar.

Jekyll's heart jumped. He ran forward. He saw him, bursting out of the mass, running forward, his arms outstretched.

"Hyde!" Jekyll screamed.

Jekyll's eyes met with Hyde's, and then Jekyll looked at the rising bridge. "Run, dear Hyde, run!"

Hyde sprinted toward the moat. His toes touched the precipice and he leaped through the air. Jekyll lost his breath as he watched Hyde sail above the moat, and, in a terrible instant, realize that Hyde wasn't going to make it.

The top half of Hyde's body landed on the front of the bridge and he slid back, clawing at the wood-en planks.

"Hyde!" Jekyll shrieked. He ran to the bridge.

The mob stopped at the moat and started throwing rocks and sticks at Hyde, who dangled from the tip of the rising bridge.

"Jekyll! Help!" Hyde shouted.

Jekyll clamored up the bridge, losing his footing and falling back and then climbing again until he reached the top. Hyde cried out. He slipped closer to the edge, losing his grip. He looked down and saw the millions of piranha swimming beneath him in the moat. He wondered what it was going to be like to die. And then Hyde felt strong hands on his wrists pulling him forward and upward. He wiggled and grabbed Jekyll's arms. The bridge went higher. Jekyll pulled. He yelled. He pulled harder. Hyde held on. The mob cried out for blood. The bridge groaned. Hyde's knees hit the tip of the bridge. Jekyll fell backward, pulling Hyde along with him and they tumbled to the bottom of the bridge in each other's arms.

Jekyll and Hyde looked into each other's eyes.

"You saved me," Hyde said.

"You came back," Jekyll said.

Oblivious to the world, they smiled, closed their eyes, and kissed.

☺

"Kill the freaks! Kill the freaks!" The mob chanted.

Hand in hand, Jekyll and Hyde ran back to join

their friends. The Awesome Authors of Super Scary Stories of Dover, NH watched in horror as the mob wheeled out a catapult.

"Where the hell did they get that?!" Jeff shouted, echoing the group's thoughts.

They watched as the mob got out the catapult's owner's manual and started reading the operating directions and discussing plans of attack.

"I hope they're slow readers," Jeff said.

"Quasimodo! Assault them with your flatulence!" Jekyll said.

Quasimodo shook his head. "Sorry man, I'm all out of gas."

"What shall we do?" Vic Sr. said. "Ideas anyone?"

Vic Jr. grumbled and shook his head. Everyone else raised one eyebrow and tapped their fingers on their chins. The seconds flew by.

"Nope, I got nothin'," Jeff said.

"Me either," Quasimodo admitted.

"Well, it appears that I have something," Jekyll said. He raised his arm and pointed toward the horizon. "Look, there!"

Everyone's gaze followed Jekyll's finger and they saw the words of Jekyll's novel coming up over the hill, spinning and speeding and flying toward the mob.

A cheer went up from the group of friends as Jekyll's words tore into the crowd, severing limbs, gouging out eyes, spilling guts, and giving wicked gnarly wedgies. The members of the mob ran back and forth, blinded by the blood in their eyes, crying, slamming into each other and swinging fists and fighting and cursing. The catapult suddenly went off, tossing a man and a woman high into the air. The trajectory was off and the two mobsters crashed into the face of the drawbridge and fell down into the moat. The sound of tortured screaming and frothing water rose up from the moat.

"You saved us all!" Hyde said to Jekyll.

Jekyll blushed. Hyde pulled him close and their lips pressed together. Jekyll and Hyde's friends clapped and cheered for them. Quasimodo, who is a hopeless romantic, wiped a tear from his eye.

A surge of pure love erupted from Jekyll and Hyde and shot out across the moat. The love struck the ground underneath the mob. A powerful quake shook the earth! The ground split open. The people of the mob cried out as they fell, one by one, into the dark pit and the earth swallowed them away.

Jekyll and Hyde reached out to Jeff, Quasimodo, Vic Sr., and Vic Jr. With smiles all around, the friends drew in close for a group hug, and across the moat, the sound of the mob faded away.

Jekyll looked up and saw the words from his manuscript swirling above the moat. "Thank you, Percy!" He called out. He took out his cell phone, swiped across the screen, pressed down, and the words flew up into a cloud.

"…For safe keeping," Jekyll said.

"What kind of name is Percy for a manuscript?" Vic Sr. asked.

"For God's sake, man, it's a family name!" Jekyll replied.

A roar of laughter went up from the friends as they turned and walked into the castle, the mammoth garage doors shutting behind them.

And the screen faded to black.

☺

"Well kids, that sure was a close call. For a minute there I wasn't sure if our heroes were going to make it or not!" Matt said.

"It was pretty nerve wracking!" Edward agreed, nodding his head.

The two tall brothers stood in the center of a graveyard, dressed in black, surrounded by darkness, fog, and flying bats. A pale moon loomed above them, and, in the distance, a broken Ferris wheel creaked in slow revolutions. Twisted circus music peppered with random screams played low in the background.

"I hope we all learned something important through today's show," Edward said.

"What's that, Ed?" Matt asked.

"That we all need to accept each other just as we are, and that calling people mean names is really bad," Edward answered.

"Yeah, kids, Ed here is right. Be good to each

other!"

"And brush your teeth and stay in school!" Edward added with a smile.

Matt nodded his head in agreement. "Well, looks like that's about all the time we have today, kids. Be sure to tune in next week for more scary good times on The Famous Vaughn Brothers Apocalyptic Matinee and Super Death Freak-Out Show!"

Matt and Edward raised their hands in the devil horn salute and the screen faded to black.

As the horror-themed ending credit music faded in and the credits rolled, Zachary turned to his little brother Billy, who sat next to him on the couch, his young eyes wide with wonder.

"That was so cool!" Zachary shouted, bouncing up and down with unhinged excitement. "I think that was the best episode so far!"

"Yeah!" Billy said in agreement. "When I grow up I wanna kill people with my farts, just like Quasimodo!"

"Me too! And I'm going to write a book so scary that it makes people crazy and so they fight and kill each other and I can watch and laugh!"

Billy fell back on the couch laughing. "Yeah! And we're gonna have a castle with a million piranhas and we'll feed them all the people we don't like!"

Zachary laughed and bounced on the fluffy couch cushions. Billy kicked his feet and laughed until his stomach hurt.

"TV is awesome!" Zachary exclaimed.

"Yay!" Billy shouted.

Billy gave Zachary a high-five and then they went to the kitchen to microwave a batch of super party pizza rolls as the Dover, New Hampshire public access TV logo flashed across the screen.

MEET THE AUTHORS

JODIE MANNING-BARES has been writing for over sixteen years. She began when she was twelve years old when an English teacher encouraged her to write a story for a contest. She won said contest and ended up taking both Madison county and the state of Illinois in the Young Author's Awards. Since then, she has been featured in Baum Ass Stories 2: Gayle Force and has plans to release an upcoming novel. Jodie would like to thank her husband Chaz for all the support in her writing endevours, her mother Robin, cats: Harley, Oliver, Joey, and Chloe and Kristin & Eric Will for being there and "being the best friends I could ever hope for."

DONALD ARMFIELD has things that lurk, snarl and grind their teeth running around inside his head dying to come out. Sometimes the beacon of light holding them in place blinks out and those things escape, usually during a short nap, leaking onto paper in the form of text in some weird vivid imagery. Donald is the mind behind "Hung Hounds" and "Jagermeister Walking"

He has two short story collections and a novel coming soon. Follow his page for updates. https://www.facebook.com/donald.armfield/

KEVIN CANDELA's favorite man-sized monster is the Creature from the Black Lagoon, so when the chance to contribute to this anthology came along he didn't have to ponder which "classic monster" he was going to play off with The Creature Rides Among Us. "He was a hulk by the end of the third movie," Candela says, "and he could breathe air too by that point. ONLY air, in fact. So maybe he couldn't swim back to the Amazon. Maybe he hangs out along the Sausalito coastline and eventually finds a freaky California girl of his own. And maybe they have a kid, who is pretty close to human…and a big biker type too. That was the story that wrote itself when I got wind of this project: The Creature is all about freedom, like Captain Jack Sparrow with gills, so to me riding fits him well. I can only hope I did all right wrapping a story around both a place and a culture with which I'm not personally familiar."

Candela's growing list of full length endeavors includes his Sinbad Forever series: Sinbad and the Argonauts, Sinbad at the End of the Universe and the in-work trilogy finale, Sinbad at the Dawn of Time. In addition he has done a pair of horror/sf/fantasy collections, A Year in the Borderlands and Playing With Reality; the serialized apocalyptic epic Weedeaters: The Complete Acropalypse; The Oz Files, his comic narrative based on L. Frank Baum's Wizard of Oz, the Dragon's Game Trilogy (Mushroom Summer, The Ballad of Chalice Rayne and Dragon's Game) and the just released Krakenstein Vs. Koalatron. Upcoming releases include the comic novella Nakedman: Epic Tales of Uncomfortable Adventure, about the most reluctant hero you're ever likely to meet, and Little Women with Big Guns, a Buckaroo Banzai/Big Trouble in Little China-style saga of interdimensional heroines squaring off against the dreaded Invisigoths and their fearsome queen Nihilani.

Check out Kevin's catalog at Amazon Books.

KENT HILL is the "new", thinking-man's Jean Claude Van Damme. He has been known to fight in desperate battles against impossible odds against hordes of imaginary foes. He has been known to volunteer for suicide missions, and has been witnessed shooting fireballs from his eyes and bolts of lightning from his arse. He is the author of Alien Smut Peddlers from the Future (StrangeHouse Books), DeathMaster: Adventures in the 39th Uncharted Dimension, The Last Barbarian (with Craig

Mullins), Necropolis Tryst, Zombie Park, Retirement Village of the Damned (all for Riot Forge), The Ballad of the Crying Clown in Floppy Shoes Apocalypse, Give me a home among the Zombies in Undead Legacy, The Ghost Mask in Doorway to Death, The Last of the Green Grass in Under the Bridge, Won't you be my Neighbour in Suburban Secrets, The Day the Pizza Died in JEAPers Creepers, Hercules with a Shotgun in Straight to Video, Army of Dicks in The Sequel: Straight 2 Video, Old Dave dies at the End in Drowning in Gore, That Bastard Loner in Strange Dominion, Natural Born Clerks in MvF, Little Tommy Psycho in Pyscho-Path, The Freaky Four in Freaks, Old Dave dies at the End in Drowning in Gore, (Editor) Straight to Video & The Sequel: Straight 2 Video (all anthologies for J. Ellington Ashton Press), The Man in the Hand in Destroy All Robots, Sword Dude (both for Dynatox Ministries) Hercules with a Shotgun {Cinema of Awesomeness Series}, Those the Shadows Hide in Conquest of the Planet of the Tapes: Straight to Video III and Contains Crude Language, Sword Dude 2, Outback Bites (Coming Soon) (for KHP).

He lives on "The Downs" in Southern Queensland, Australia, with his wife and son.

TOM LUCAS was born and raised in Detroit,

and although currently enjoying the lack of snow and ice in Florida, remains a son of the post-industrial apocalypse.

He is a college professor, author, blogger, poet, book reviewer, and spoken word performer.

Tom has been published in The Orlando Weekly, Writer's Digest, The Writer's Monthly Review, The South End, The Oakland Press, The Macomb Daily, Orbit, Anthropomorphic, and U. Magazine. He has also been featured in literary journals such as The Write Place at the Write Time, Graffiti Rag, F*cked Up Fairy Tales, and Dark Fire Fiction. He has performed on the Lollapalooza stage as well as guest spots on CIMX, WDET, and WJR.

When not writing, Tom likes to drive fast and take chances.

For more information visit: http://readtomlucas.com/

ROMA GRAY writes what she refers to as "Trick-or-Treat Thrillers", stories with a spooky, creepy, Halloween feel to them.

She currently has three published books: "Gray Shadows Under a Harvest Moon" (short story collection), "The Hunted Tribe: Declaration of War" (novel), and "Celebration of Horror" (short story collection), with two new novels "Jurassic Jackaroo: Jasper's Junction" and "Haunted House Harbor: Humanity's Hope" scheduled to be published in 2017. In addition to this, she has thirteen published short stories with sixteen short stories scheduled to be published over the next year. Currently she works at J. Ellington Ashton as a staff editor and Director of Marketing as well as for own editing company, Night Sky Book Services.

She lives in a haunted house in Oregon with her black cat, Chihuahua, and parrot.

Amazon Author Page:

https://www.amazon.com/Roma-Gray/e/B00UP2CU1U/ref=sr_ntt_srch_lnk_1?qid=1499300958&sr=8-1

Audible Page (audiobooks):

http://www.audible.com/search/ref=a_search_c4_1_1_1_srAuth?searchAuthor=Roma+Gray&qid=1499301156&sr=1-1

Website:

https://trickortreatthrillers.com

JONATHAN MOON is a dark fiction writer living in Moscow, Idaho. He is the twisted mind behind HEINOUS, Worms in the Needle, Hollow Mountain Dead, Stories To Poke your Eyes Out To, and several other nasty and terrible things. Recently accepted into the Masters of Anthropology program at the University of Idaho Mr. Moon plans on spending his life studying the human animal. He wears masks, carries knives, and tells lies. Lots and lots of lies.

SCOTT CLARINGBOLD lives with his wife and daughter in the very north of England, a stones throw from the Scottish border. His son is now his own man and lives in York with his girlfriend. In November 2016 Scott's first published story, Coma, appeared in The Show Must Go On (a collection of short stories celebrating the life of Freddie Mercury). In 2017, Scott edited Nine Lives - a Doctor Who charity anthology raising money for charity. He also contributed to Baum Ass 2: Gayle Force for Riot Forge and The Unofficial Doctor Who Limerick Book for Long Scarf Productions. More stories are due to appear in the next year, including the Super-villain anthology Palookaville from Pine Float Press.

MICHELLE GARZA and **MELISSA LASON** are a twin sister writing team from Arizona. Their work has been published by Sinister Grin Press, Dark Fuse and Pint bottle Press. Their debut novel, Mayan Blue, was nominated for a Bram Stoker Award for superior achievement in a first novel for 2016.

ESSEL PRATT is a master of horror and fantasy, conjuring tales that haunt souls and inspire imagination. As a student of psychology and teller of tales, Essel writes to share the complex nature of his imaginings with the world. His ever-expanding catalog of short stories spans multiple anthologies and collections, ranging from whimsical fantasy to bizarre horror, including everything in between. Dedicated fans have praised his creations, labeling his talents as prolific in substance.

Hailing from Mishawaka, Indiana, his passion for writing began in the early years as his imagination taunted from within, begging for a release. Dabbling in art at first, he found that the stories that pleaded to be told could not be imprisoned by ink and paint alone. His most notable and prevalent accomplishments include Final Reverie, Sharkantula, and the multiple short stories that have garnered a following of their own, such as the adventures of Detective Mansfield.

Inspired by C.S. Lewis, Clive Barker, Stephen King, Harper Lee, William Golding, and many more, Essel doesn't restrain his writings to straight horror, instead exploring the blurred boundaries of horror within its competing genres, mixing the elements into a literary stew.

You can follow Essel at the following:
www.facebook.com/esselprattwriting
Esselpratt.blogspot.com
@EsselPratt
http://esselpratt.wixsite.com/darknessbreaks

When he's not defending humanity against giant insects, **SCOTT ERICKSON** is an award-winning writer of humor and satire. He feels at home in Portland, Oregon, which has the largest roller skating rink west of the Mississippi River and the highest concentration of craft beer breweries in America. More information can be found at www.scott-erickson-writer.com

RUSSELL HOLBROOK's love for monsters and the macabre began at an early age. He wrote his first splattastic Horror story in the second grade and never looked back, except that one time when his head spun around backwards and he spewed green slime on his teacher. Just kidding, unfortunately that didn't actually happen; he just threw up on her shoes. His writing has been featured in multiple Horror and Bizarro anthologies and he has released two novellas: Joy (Riot Forge) and, The Water Babies (SlashHouse Fiction). He is currently hard at work on his first full-length novel, banging away on the keyboard at his home in Mableton, Georgia. Aside from writing Russell is also a musician and visual artist. He welcomes your questions, comments, and gifts of tater tots and veggie burgers. Please get in touch via the following:

https://www.facebook.com/russell.holbrook.5

https://harmonylull.bandcamp.com/

https://vimeo.com/user1661659

https://www.amazon.com/Russell-Holbrook/e/B01M3VJW72/ref=dp_byline_cont_ebooks_1

MEET THE EDITORS

MATTHEW VAUGHN is the author of The ADHD Vampire from Bizarro Pulp Press and Mother F'ing Black Skull of Death from Morbidbooks. He lives in Shelbyville, Kentucky and is the father of four little children, yet he and his wife are just big kids too. By day he maintains machines and robots, by night he is a writer of Bizarro and Horror fiction. You can keep up with his work at

http://mcvaughn.wordpress.com

https://www.facebook.com/AuthorMatthewVaughn/

EDWARD VAUGHN is a horror and crime fiction writer from Louisville, Kentucky. He has had stories seen in Baum Ass Tales 2, Sanitarium Magazine, Near To The Knuckle, and Shotgun Honey. Follow him on Twitter at DawnOfThe_Ed and his blog Red All Over on Wordpress.

Made in the USA
Lexington, KY
05 December 2017